SPACE PIRATES!
BOOK II

DEAD MEN LAUNCH NO SHIPS

MARK VOSS

BAL
KON
media

DEAD MEN LAUNCH NO SHIPS
Published by Balkon Media

Paperback edition ISBN: 978-1-916970-45-8
Also available as an E-book

A CIP catalogue record for this title is available from the British Library.

Cover Design: Balkon Media

www.vossiverse.com

ALSO BY MARK VOSS

THE SPACE PIRATES! SERIES

Space Pirates

Dead Men Launch No Ships

Salvage Rights

Echoes of the Plague Moon

The Quiet Rebellion

The Bounty Paradox

The Black Drift

Till the Engines Fall Silent

The Median Gambit

ONE

The Meridian was a ship built for three things: running from creditors, leaking coolant, and making the concept of "routine maintenance" sound like a threat. At the farthest point of the Halcyon Fringe, it floated with the lazy self-confidence of a vessel that had survived more catastrophic failures than most ships logged in their entire service lives. Its hull bore the scars of three forced-boardings and at least one bankruptcy tribunal. The main galley—such as it was—smelled of burnt coffee, cold metal, and something that might, in better circumstances, be described as victory.

Lyra had wedged herself in the primary access hatch, boots off, bare feet braced against opposite bulkheads. There was an empty mug perched on her knee and a full one in her hand, the brew inside black enough to nullify light. Her hair was clipped so short it barely counted, and the only part of her uniform that could be called "regulation" was the oil stain spreading with an almost geological patience across her left thigh. She sipped her coffee and eyed the line of the starboard pressure readouts, watching for the tell-tale twitch of a vacuum leak. It wasn't that she distrusted the ship's diagnostics—she simply preferred to see disaster coming.

Across the galley, Mercy had commandeered the battered table, which was losing its war against both gravity and numerous impromptu repairs. She sorted credit chips into precise columns, flicking them with the neat aggression of a casino croupier. Her hair was currently fuchsia with violent green streaks, and the battered boots propped on the next chair over looked like they'd been through a minor war—if said war had a dress code for maximal insubordination. She counted aloud, voice thick with the sort of mischief that only comes from recently coming into some money.

"One for me," Mercy said, sliding a chip into a tiny pile, "one for repairs, and one for the captain's next terrible idea." She repeated the cycle with increasing satisfaction. "One for me. One for Lyra. One for criminally poor judgement."

Behind the main console, Rask Helvan contributed a tuneless hum to the room's atmosphere. It was unclear whether he was actually working or just waiting for the next crisis to present itself. Rask wore his ancient flight jacket like a second skin, and even with his feet up and hands behind his head, he gave the impression of someone about to con a customs inspector or steal an airlock. His hair was just this side of presentable, and the left eyebrow had a permanent upward tilt, like it suspected the rest of his face was in on a joke and refusing to explain it.

He pecked at the console with a single finger, muttering numbers under his breath. "Good news, crew: We are solvent. Technically. Briefly. But definitely solvent."

Lyra took another drink. "Define solvent."

Rask grinned, white teeth flashing against three days of stubble. "If you ignore essential repairs, fuel, docking, outstanding warrants, and the entire concept of taxes, we're basically aristocrats."

Mercy whistled, then swept the chips off the table into a lumpy pouch. "You hear that, Lyra? We're aristocrats. Better start practicing your sneer."

"Was already ahead of you," Lyra said, deadpan. She straightened and jabbed a finger at a distant readout. "By the way, portside coil's running at twelve percent over spec. Either the diagnostics are hallucinating or we're about to burn a hole in the manifold. Again."

Doc materialised with the silent disapproval of a man who'd seen too many of these mornings. His white coat was only recognisable as such by its persistent failure to combust during routine engine fires, and his hands carried the faint chemical tang of antiseptics. He set a battered medkit on the galley counter and regarded the scene with a look that could have curdled milk.

"Should we alert the authorities?" Doc said, already rifling through the kit to see what had gone missing since yesterday.

"Don't joke," Rask said. "We might actually have to see a customs officer on this run."

Lyra raised her mug in a toast. "May all your lies be small and plausible."

Doc shot her a look of professional respect, then went back to counting bandages. "Who left a femoral clamp in the fridge?" he said to no one in particular.

Mercy's head snapped up. "That's where it went! Technically, I was keeping it cold for science."

"I'm certain that's how infection control works," Doc replied, and stowed the clamp in the kit without breaking eye contact.

The intercom crackled to life with a low, mechanical sigh. Then: "Captain Rask Helvan has successfully completed a job and did not explode. Historians will want the exact date. Suggest commemorative plaque." The voice was feminine, with the dry, sing-song intonation of a children's AI that had grown up around far too many war stories and drunk uncles using bad language.

Mercy craned her neck at the nearest speaker. "Glim, was that a compliment?"

The AI's reply came with a faint electronic purr. "Not for you."

Mercy made a theatrical show of heartbreak, pressing a hand to her chest. "I feel so neglected, Glim. I might sabotage the air supply."

"Please do. I am bored," Glim said, then dropped the line with a snap.

Lyra looked up at the ceiling. "Can we get a new ship intelligence?"

Rask shook his head. "Too late. The last one's still sending legal threats." He swivelled the chair to face his crew, folding his hands behind his head. "I propose a brief celebration, and then we get ahead of our next disaster."

Mercy already had a packet of something orange and carcinogenic open. She offered it around. "Celebrate what, specifically?"

Rask's grin sharpened. "We finished a job, we got paid, and the authorities haven't impounded us. What more do you want?"

Mercy thought for a moment, then shrugged. "Sex, booze, violence. The classics."

"Pick two," Lyra said.

Mercy gave her a sly look. "Not enough time for all three?"

Doc, who'd been reorganising the medkit by triage order, set it down with a little more force than necessary. "If you're going to have sex or violence, warn me first. I can only stitch so fast."

The bridge of the Meridian was a study in controlled neglect. There were three seats: one for the pilot, one for the engineer, and one for a person who didn't care about living past the next hyperspace jump. Rask, who filled all three roles interchangeably, currently had his boots up on the console and a mug of Lyra's brew balanced perilously on his knee. He was just about to attempt the impossible —drinking it without using his hands—when Glim's voice cut through the hum of systems in that way only impending catastrophe could.

"Incoming transmission," Glim said. "Origin: pre-

War bandwidth. Translation difficulty: ninety-seven percent. Tone: ominous."

Mercy was first to react. She'd sprawled across the co-pilot seat, boots scraping chips of dried sealant off the armrest, and she perked up like a dog that smelled fresh explosives. "Pre-War? Isn't that the bandwidth they reserved for imperial command?"

"Supposedly," Glim replied, already huffy. "But it's not in my records. That makes me uncomfortable."

Doc drifted in, mug in one hand, medscanner in the other, and took up residence behind Rask's shoulder. "Probably a trap," he said, as if reading tomorrow's weather.

Rask, for his part, looked delighted. "Or a payday that's been waiting for someone exactly this stupid." He leaned in, eyes narrowing as the console filled with a crawling string of corrupted data—pixels twitching like a dying lizard.

Lyra's voice, equal parts caffeine and challenge, came from the hatch as she strode in and checked the readouts. "That format shouldn't exist."

"Most of our ship shouldn't exist," Doc pointed out. "Yet here we are."

Glim piped up again, "Shall I ignore the message, or is the prevailing mood 'run directly toward possible doom?'"

Mercy sat up, already grinning. "Glim, I knew you were starting to get us."

Rask drummed fingers on the console. "Let's see what the dead have to say."

The main screen flickered. A pattern emerged—three

slow, deliberate pulses of static, followed by an echoing digital silence. Lyra stared at the waveform, brow furrowing. "That's a distress call. Or a summons. The format's close, but there's a layer under it—encrypted, maybe. Glim?"

"Working on it," Glim replied, and the console lit up with ghostly overlays—strings of Imperial ciphers and ancient military signets that shimmered at the edge of comprehension.

Doc sipped his drink and made a face. "Why would anyone broadcast from a dead protocol? No one's supposed to be listening."

Rask's gaze sharpened. "Unless they want to be found by someone who'd know how."

Mercy bobbed her head. "Whoever it is, they know us, or people like us."

Lyra rolled her eyes. "If it's a bounty, it'll be ten years past expiry. We might actually owe money for showing up."

Glim interrupted: "I have cross-referenced the source. Plotting on the nav overlay."

A vector painted itself across the star chart, ending at a thin cluster of dust and rock labelled "Filt Region – Decommissioned."

"Nothing out there but wrecks and bad luck," Lyra said.

Mercy leaned in, too close to the display. "So... standard working conditions."

Doc muttered, "Only if we get paid in advance."

Glim ran a diagnostic and projected it over the main viewport: a single point, faint, oscillating. "Signal integrity is deteriorating. Source is in decay orbit. Recommend immediate investigation, for values of 'recommend' that also mean 'beg.'"

Rask looked from the screen to his crew, then back again. "I vote we go. Worst case, we get a story for the next time someone tries to drink us under the table."

Mercy pumped a fist. "Let's die legendary."

Lyra shrugged. "I'll plot an approach, but if this turns into another unpaid job, I'm holding you personally responsible."

"That's the spirit," Rask said, standing to stretch. He was grinning like a man who'd just been handed the keys to a forbidden room and intended to touch everything inside.

Doc rolled his eyes, but didn't argue. "I'll prep for trauma."

The ship banked as Lyra keyed in a course correction, the Meridian responding with its usual catalogue of complaints—shivering through the struts, a groan from the bulkhead, and the stench of overworked life-support. The dust sector grew in the viewport, starfield thinning as they accelerated toward the anomaly.

On the main screen, the signal repeated—three faint beats, so regular they sounded like the pulse of a long-dead heart.

Mercy watched it, rapt. "Anyone else get the feeling we're being invited to our own funeral?"

Rask grinned wider, eyes reflecting the blue-white of the ghostly transmission. "Maybe. But the food's always good at these things."

Lyra shook her head, mouth twitching in what might have been a smile. "You are incapable of caution."

"I prefer the term 'allergic,'" Rask replied. "But sometimes I mean well."

Glim's digital sigh made the overheads flicker. "Plotting course to our inevitable demise. Arrival in four hours, thirty-six minutes."

Doc checked the medscanner, already resigned. "Odds on what's waiting for us?"

Mercy didn't hesitate. "Angry warlord. Or one of those spooky cyborg cults that believe in enlightenment through pain. Ooh, or a rescue pod full of gold."

"My money's on derelict. Maybe a corpse. Maybe several," Lyra ventured.

"You are all wrong," Glim said. "But I am not authorised to say how."

The console crackled as the message played one last time. Three beats, a breath, and then a single word burned through the static:

VIGILANCE

The Meridian held course, every eye on the ghost in the machine. No one blinked.

No one wanted to be the first to admit they were afraid.

TWO

Meridian's transition out of sublight always came with a minor existential jolt, like waking to realise the universe was still fundamentally broken but at least you'd made it through the night. The main viewport flickered and resettled, painting the Halcyon Fringe in a litter of ancient light and scorched rock.

Lyra flicked her gaze from the sensors to the external feeds, unimpressed by the scale of the debris field. It wasn't so much a navigational hazard as a case study in orbital neglect. "You'd think if the Empire had the resources to build a ship like that," she said, "they'd clean up after themselves."

"Or just leave a sternly worded sign," Doc replied, peering over her shoulder. "Warning: Contains dead dreams and loose bolts."

Mercy pressed in, eyes fixed on the growing dark blot at the edge of the dust belt. "That's her, then. The Vigilance. Looks bigger up close."

The sensor overlay did not do the warship justice. At

this range, the vessel stretched across half the viewport, even with most of its hull lost to battle, time, or both. The outer plates were warped, scorched and stitched with impacts that had clearly ignored all known conventions for civilised warfare. Cold engines gaped at the void, blackened and rimed in a crust of extruded insulation. Whatever had once powered Vigilance, it had either fled or died spectacularly.

But the hull was the real monument: half a kilometre of composite armour, banded with cooling veins and redundant conduits that had once, presumably, kept thousands of souls alive and productive. Now, the insignia along the midline was pitted and abraded— "IMPERIAL EXECUTIVE COMMAND"—the words eroded into a barely legible sneer.

A faint blue pulse shimmered along the ship's spinal core. It wasn't strong enough to illuminate, but every minute or so the line glowed, rippling down the hull like a nerve remembering it should have been alive. The effect was less lifeline, more corpse twitch.

"That's not a ship," Lyra said, adjusting the spectrum. "That's a mausoleum."

Mercy gave a low whistle. "Still counts as salvage."

Doc folded his arms, lip curling. "Unless the ghosts charge rent."

On cue, Glim's voice drifted through the overheads: "VIGILANCE – COMMAND-CLASS WARSHIP, DECOMMISSIONED 22 YEARS AGO." She let the silence stretch, then added, "Survived six major conflicts, not including the legal aftermath. No living crew listed in recent records."

Rask drifted in, just awake enough to look like he'd been up for hours. He took in the scene with that half-lidded amusement reserved for professional disasters. "Someone really wanted to make a point," he said. "Any indication of why it's still ticking?"

Lyra scrolled through the diagnostics. "Half the power grid is shot. The other half is—" she squinted "—cycling between blackout and some sort of locked-down restart."

Mercy tapped the display. "Maybe it's haunted. Wouldn't be the weirdest job we've had."

"Wouldn't even make top five," Doc said.

Rask grinned, showing teeth. "Come on, admit it. You're all a little curious."

"No," said Lyra. Then, after a beat, "Yes, but only as a professional courtesy."

The ship shivered as Lyra rolled the Meridian into a slow, cautious flyby. Hull sensors pinged off chunks of burnt metal and, once, the dense core of what might have been an escape pod, now fused into a single piece of celestial litter.

Rask squinted at the feed. "Glim, you see any active defences?"

A pause, then: "If there are any left, they're pointed at each other."

He shrugged. "Less work for us, then."

Lyra tracked the blue pulse as it jittered down the warship's centreline. "It's running a loop. I can't get a fix, but something in the core is still drawing."

Doc muttered, "Powering what, exactly? The lights?"

Mercy, eyes bright, said, "Maybe it's got one of those doomsday vaults. We could retire on the resale value."

Lyra deadpanned, "Or it's venting reactor coolant and we'll all die of cosmic cancer."

Mercy's grin only widened. "That's why we bring Doc."

Doc sighed and shook his head. "I'm a physician, not a Geiger counter."

They banked for a closer pass. The Meridian's forward floodlights cut across Vigilance's flanks, illuminating new scars: docking rings torn open, extruded cabling looped around the hull like the ship's own entrails. There were places where fire had welded corridor doors straight through, locking half the bulkheads in a permanent clench.

And then there was the flag.

It clung to the dorsal antenna, stiff as a board, its Imperial sigil still visible through the frost. The flag was snapped in mid-motion—caught as it tried and failed to escape. Lyra stared at it for a moment, feeling the oddest prick of sympathy.

Glim, ever the mood-breaker, piped in: "I've found the control registry. It's broadcasting on an open channel, but only to local comms. There's a repeating handshake request."

Mercy immediately replied, "Should I say hi?"

Doc snorted. "You'll end up married to the autopilot."

Mercy smirked. "Wouldn't be my first."

Rask ignored them, eyes on the main display. "Patch us in, Glim. Let's see if the thing wants to negotiate."

The speakers rattled with a burst of static, then a voice—thin, mechanical, and precisely modulated—echoed through the bridge.

"Helvan. Meridian. You are in violation of Imperial salvage protocol. Stand by for retrieval."

Lyra arched an eyebrow. "That's not a warning. That's a boarding action."

Rask looked unbothered. "Then it's a good thing we're not worth boarding."

"Or a bad thing, if it means they're bored," Mercy said.

Glim, with evident relish: "The good news is, I've found no signs of life. The bad news is, I've also found no signs of death. Make of that what you will."

Lyra felt a ripple of unease, not that she'd admit it. She keyed in a passive scan, watching the energy patterns flicker in and out of coherence like a stubborn fever.

Rask leaned back and kicked his feet up on the edge of the console, every inch the man at home in a disaster. "Set us into a holding pattern. Let's get the lay of the decks before we start poking inside."

Mercy took the controls. "We staying out of tractor range?"

Rask shrugged. "If it has one left, I want to see what happens."

Doc rolled his eyes. "Last time you wanted to see what happened, we spent two weeks eating nothing but hydroponic beetroot."

"That's character-building," Rask said, unrepentant. "Besides, Glim was getting bored."

Glim's lights flickered an icy blue. "Now I am merely existentially perturbed."

As the Meridian coasted, Lyra watched the Vigilance roll slowly beneath them. One of the docking rings hung open, teeth bared to the void. The pulse along the ship's spine quickened, for just a moment, as if the whole vessel was trying to remember what it meant to be alive.

Lyra muttered, "Never seen anything like it."

Mercy, almost reverent: "She's beautiful. In a homicidal kind of way."

Doc just shook his head. "You people need hobbies."

For a long minute, they sat in silence, the warship rotating below, the distant stars uncaring.

Rask, softly: "All right, crew. Who wants to go say hello?"

No one answered, but no one protested either.

The Meridian circled in for another pass, lights sweeping the Vigilance, as if hoping the old battleship would blink first.

It didn't.

There was a special kind of dread reserved for boarding derelicts: too old to be dangerous, too new to be truly dead. The Meridian's airlock had a ritual to it—check seals, count heads, remember to bring someone expendable. In this case, expendable meant Rask, Lyra, Mercy, and Doc.

Glim piped up in their helmets, tinny and officious: "Shuttle trajectory stable. You are now statistically more likely to die in a tragic accident than by random violence. Congratulations."

"Achievement unlocked," Rask muttered, flexing his gloves. He checked the tether harness twice, mostly for show.

Lyra was already keyed into the airlock's control matrix. "Remote sequence set. We have exactly four minutes before this corridor cycles back to hard vacuum, so everyone keep your prayers brief."

Mercy looked delighted. "Does suffocating count as a crisis, or just a career highlight?"

Doc, bringing up the rear, let out a sigh that steamed inside his helmet. "Just once, I'd like to patch up someone who got hurt by something normal. A blender, say."

The external corridor linking Meridian to Vigilance was a stretch of vacuum-welded conduit, officially rated for industrial cargo but long ago repurposed for less legal activities. Every fifteen metres, a battered luminaire flickered in and out of relevance, casting the tethered figures in staccato shadow. The far end was a mouth—Vigilance's primary dorsal airlock, sealed shut by Imperial overkill and then left to rot by neglect.

Glim monitored their approach, running commentary as they crossed. "Radiation at corridor midline is elevated. Suggest holding your breath until I say otherwise."

Mercy took the lead, jetting from handhold to handhold, boots barely touching the mesh. "Bet you fifty credits I make it to the lock before Lyra."

"Easy money," Lyra shot back. "I don't want to get there first."

Doc, voice flat: "If you both get there at the same time, can you at least die in a dignified manner?"

They made the crossing in record time, not because they wanted to, but because the void behind them felt less comforting than the haunted hulk ahead.

Lyra reached the airlock panel, wiped the frost from its surface, and set to work. She pulled a stubby multitool from her belt and levered open a maintenance port with clinical violence. The inner workings were old, hand-labelled in a script that suggested either paranoia or poor eyesight.

"Imperial safety standards," she grumbled. "Still terrible."

She jumped a pair of contacts, kicked the reset, and the lock shuddered. Mercy leaned over her shoulder, offering helpful advice: "Try hitting it harder."

Lyra glared, then did.

The door responded with a hiss, more petulant than mechanical, and drifted open by degrees. The first whiff of air was less a smell than a texture—oily and metallic. It made Rask's nose itch inside the helmet.

"Permission to enter," Glim intoned, then, "Please note: first to cross threshold assumes all legal liability for subsequent curses."

Mercy barrelled through, boots first.

Inside, Vigilance was a cathedral for the terminally disappointed. The corridor curved gently away from the lock, lined in black polymer and edged with icy lattice where atmosphere had frozen on cold steel. Every three steps, the gravity shifted—one moment a gentle tug, next a leap that sent boots scraping the ceiling.

Lyra's breath fogged the inside of her visor as she walked. "Gravity's at a third. Either the backup's failing or this ship ran on optimism."

Doc trailed them, medical bag clipped to his hip. "I've seen worse," he said, then corrected himself: "No, wait, I haven't."

Mercy ran a finger along the wall, then looked at it. "Steel's holding. No corrosion."

"You say that like it's good news," Doc said.

They moved deeper, each step met by the faintest echo of themselves—like the ship wanted to remember what it was like to be full. The only light came from irregular emergency strips, their intervals just wrong enough to set nerves on edge.

Rask brought up the rear, glancing into every side chamber. Most were sealed, a few open to reveal banks of equipment, all inert. It was a museum of failure.

Glim's voice returned, lower and more subdued: "I am picking up sporadic electrical activity. It's not enough to run the life support, but it's definitely... trying."

"Trying to do what?" Rask asked.

"Impossible to say. But if it starts talking to you directly, let me know."

They rounded a curve and found themselves at the threshold of the command antechamber. In better days, it would have hummed with status reports and discipline. Now, the only motion was the slow drift of particles through a beam of emergency light.

The consoles were dead, all except for one: a skeletal holo-projector perched atop a cracked command desk. The image flickered, looping a single line of text:

LOCKSTEP INITIATION: STANDBY

Lyra stopped short. "That's not a distress signal. That's a boot sequence."

Mercy peered closer. "Anyone know what a lockstep is?"

Doc looked at Rask. "Sounds like a military thing."

Rask's lips thinned. "Means someone—or something —is trying to wake up."

They stood in a silence thick with regret. Only Mercy broke it, reaching out to poke the display.

As her glove passed through the hologram, the emergency lighting dipped, then rebounded brighter. From somewhere deeper in the ship, a clang reverberated—a single note that seemed to come from everywhere at once.

All four froze.

Glim's voice cut through the tension, uncharacteristically urgent: "Sensors just picked up residual heat from Cryo Deck 3."

Mercy's hand went to her sidearm. "Define residual."

"I'd love to," Glim replied, "but it's moving."

Rask gestured for the team to fan out—a gesture made difficult by the fact that no one actually wanted to leave his shadow. They advanced down the next corridor, weapons drawn, lights sweeping in a deliberate arc.

The air grew colder, and the frost thickened. Ahead, the cryo bay door stood slightly ajar, its surface pocked with impact scars. Mercy took point, nudged the door with her boot, and let it swing open.

The bay was a cavern, lined floor to ceiling with glass-fronted sarcophagi. Most were empty, cracked or shattered. A few were still misted, shadows moving within.

One of those shadows moved in a way that didn't belong to any sleep cycle. It pushed against the glass, slow and deliberate, then retracted as if considering. Frost peeled from the inside as a hand—human, but grey and bruised—dragged across.

"Eyes up," Lyra whispered.

A hiss of pneumatics, then the door on pod seventeen shuddered open.

The figure inside fell forward, hitting the deck hard. Frost steamed off battered armour, the insignia long scorched into anonymity. The helmet twisted free and clattered away.

Mercy swore softly. Doc made a noise halfway between disgust and clinical interest. Lyra raised her gun.

The woman on the deck blinked into the torchlight—smaller, leaner, but unmistakable. Same sharp jaw. Same scar under the left eye. Same expression that said she'd already judged them all and found them lacking.

She was Rask in every way that counted—the same features, the same bearing, the same eyes—only female, as though the Empire had built him again and corrected the design.

Rask stared, speechless.

The woman's lips parted, voice hoarse but chillingly familiar.

"Captain... you came back."

Rask's mouth went dry. The pitch was higher, but the cadence—the tone—was his own. Every syllable precise. Controlled. Condescending.

Mercy whispered, "It's a clone. Right? Please tell me it's a clone."

Doc didn't lower his weapon. "Or an identity crisis in progress.

The woman braced a hand against the deck and pushed herself upright. Her movements were slow, careful—like a machine relearning its limits. She stood half a head shorter than Rask, but the stare levelled him just the same

"I am... unfinished," she said. "You left me here."

Rask finally found his voice. "I've never seen you in my life."

She smiled without humour. "You say that as though it matters."

Behind her, rows of cryo pods blinked from red to amber. The air filled with a slow, mechanical heartbeat—fans spinning, hydraulics cycling.

Lyra's grip tightened. "Pods are going active. We need to move."

Glim's voice crackled through the comms, precise as ever. "Captain, thermal readings increasing across the bay. The other pods are in partial wake sequence. Recommend strategic retreat."

Mercy's eyes swept the room. "Define strategic."

"Leaving," said Glim. "Immediately."

Rask took a half-step closer to the clone. "Who are you?"

Her eyes met his, the same grey-green as his own.

"Designation Rho. Lockstep Command Unit Two-Seven-One. Continuity failsafe."

A pause, then quieter: "You. But better."

Lyra snorted. "I'll pass."

Rho staggered, hand pressed to her abdomen. Steam curled off her armour. "System instability. Need... recalibration." Her voice trembled, breaking from military crispness to raw human strain. "If I shut down, others wake. Chain... failsafe."

Doc crouched beside her, scanner flickering. "She's not lying. She's networked into the whole system."

Lyra frowned. "Explain in sentences."

"If she dies," said Doc, "they wake up."

Mercy muttered, "Of course she's booby-trapped. Why wouldn't she be?"

"Captain?" Glim again. "Energy surge in cryo systems. Nine pods entering prime cycle. You have approximately ninety seconds before the entire room develops opinions."

Lyra swung her weapon toward the nearest pod. "I can fix that."

"Negative," said Rask. "We shoot one, we wake the rest."

"Then what?" Mercy snapped.

Rask hesitated—the moment stretching, every decision suddenly wrong. Then he exhaled, sharp and resigned. "We take her."

Lyra blinked. "We what?"

"She's the key to this," Rask said. "She's the only thing awake in this graveyard. If we leave her, those things wake. If we take her, maybe they don't."

Doc was already moving, hypospray in hand. "Mec sedative. She won't last five minutes conscious."

Rho looked up, half-dazed. "Permission... to accompany you, Captain."

Rask's throat tightened. "Yeah," he said softly. "Granted."

Doc hit her with a shot from the hypospray and she began to wobble, eyes rolling back.

Mercy slung her rifle and hauled the limp clone onto her shoulder with a grunt. "If she shoots me in my sleep, I'm haunting you."

"Get in line," Rask muttered.

They moved fast, boots thudding across frost-slick decking. Behind them, the amber pod lights flickered— the cryo bay beginning to breathe.

Glim's voice sharpened. "Recommend haste. The derelict's power grid just woke up."

"Add it to the list," Lyra said, covering the rear. "Doc, how's Sleeping Beauty?"

"Stable-ish," Doc said. "Vitals good. Sanity questionable."

"Fits right in," Mercy muttered.

As they reached the end of the corridor before it turned towards the airlock, Rask risked one last glance back at the pods—rows of his own face, dreaming under glass. Each one could wake. Each one could follow.

He hit the hatch control. "Let's get the hell out of my nightmares."

The door sealed behind them.

Moments later, the Meridian peeled away from the

Vigilance, engines flaring cold blue against the dark. The derelict drifted, silent again—for now.

Inside, pod seventeen's indicator light blinked from green back to amber, then red.

And somewhere deep within the ship, something else woke up and listened.

THREE

If there was an award for Most Overcrowded Med Bay, the Meridian would have claimed it and set it on fire for the insurance. Rask had insisted the room be "multipurpose." Lyra had translated this as "barely fit for purpose." Doc simply called it a war crime against healthcare.

At this moment, every centimetre was in use. The new arrival—the duplicate, the thing in the imperial frost suit—occupied the single working table. Doc was hunched over her, scanner in one hand, the other making compulsive notes on a splintered tablet. Cryo steam rose from the clone's armour and condensed on the overheads, forming sticky droplets that plinked onto the battered medical kit below.

Lyra, arms folded, wedged herself into the only clear space by the back wall. She hadn't left her boots at the door, on the principle that no one bled out faster from socked feet. She watched Doc work, eyes narrowed, silently tracking the speed with which he went from "reluctant" to "morbidly fascinated."

Rask paced a worn groove between the crash cart and the supply locker, boots thumping the deck with an impatience that bordered on performance art. He glanced at the clone every third step, as if expecting her to sit up and declare the whole thing a very elaborate joke.

Mercy, for once, hovered in the corridor, denied access until Doc finished his "initial autopsy on the living," which Mercy said was discriminatory against the recently thawed.

The subject herself lay inert, limbs splayed at angles suggesting both rigidity and collapse. From a distance, she could have been sleeping. Closer up, she looked like the prelude to an electrical fire.

Doc muttered to himself as he scanned her skull. "Baseline human. Grossly so. But the bone density is... right, that's not a decimal point error, that's just creative. Implants in the sternum, nanofiber overlays at major joints." He shifted the scanner to her arm, where streaks of grey ran under the skin. "Muscle augmentation, civilian grade but—" He shook his head. "Not civilian. This is custom. Somebody had a budget and a grievance."

Lyra's voice cut the air. "How's the DNA?"

Doc blinked, as if surprised she'd noticed. "Odd."

"Define odd."

He flipped the tablet and angled it so even Rask, who only believed in biology as it related to processing alcohol, could see. "See how this sequence here is stabilising —normal, standard, predictable." He tapped the screen, shifting to a new pattern. "But this is... changing itself."

Lyra arched an eyebrow. "That's not supposed to happen."

"It's not," Doc said, almost gleeful. "It's splicing in real time. Whoever grew her did not believe in genetic consistency."

Rask came to a dead halt, arms folded, expression somewhere between concern and poorly disguised horror. "So, she's a clone?"

Doc exhaled. "Not just a clone, Captain. She's a masterpiece of bad ethics."

The med bay's overhead comm pinged, then Glim's voice filtered in, annoyingly chipper for a shipboard AI. "Would you like the specifics, or the horror summary?"

"Both," Rask said, voice flat.

Glim didn't miss a beat. "Genetic analysis complete. Subject matches Captain Helvan at ninety-three percent. Margin of error: negligible. Conclusion: probable derivative or direct clone. Congratulations, Captain. You're a parent."

Silence clotted in the room. Lyra's lips twitched at the corners; Rask's jaw worked, then failed to deliver a word.

"Say that again," he managed at last.

Glim obliged, looping the report for effect. "Genetic profile is a near-perfect match. It's a copy with slight improvements in musculoskeletal, cardiovascular, and neural domains. Most notably, the subject lacks your more... whimsical alleles. Sorry, Captain. They cut out the bits that make you fun at parties."

Lyra let out a low whistle. "Oh, this is going to be hilarious."

Doc only looked up when his scanner started beeping an epileptic warning. "She's coming up to temp faster than expected. That's... impossible. Should be unconscious for hours yet."

Rask circled the table, peering at the face—a face that, if you scraped away the bruises and frostbite, looked like his own, only less tired and less likely to con you out of your boots.

He tried a smile. "Anyone else getting the urge to kill it with fire, or is that just me?"

Before anyone could reply, Mercy stormed in, a containment sleeve dangling from her hand. She looked from Doc to the table to Rask and back, then smirked. "You left the patient's sidearm in the bay. You're welcome." She held up the sleeve, which shimmered with containment fields. "It tried to shoot me, by the way."

Doc snatched the sleeve, squinted at the weapon, and snorted. "It's not even loaded."

Mercy grinned. "Then it's an optimist."

Lyra uncrossed her arms and leaned in for a closer look. "You get any reading off her brain?" she asked Doc.

He hesitated. "Depends. You want the plausible or the unsettling?"

Rask said, "Give us the unsettling. That's been the theme."

Doc angled the scanner over the clone's skull, then projected the results onto the main med bay screen. "See the spikes? That's standard for REM or high-adrenaline wake cycles. But the pattern isn't random—look here." He zoomed in, revealing an overlay of jagged, almost geometric pulses. "There's repetition. A loop. She's not dreaming—she's processing."

Lyra frowned. "Processing what?"

"Encrypted data," Glim interjected. "Pattern matches Imperial tactical burst protocol. It's a memory relay, not a dream state."

Rask looked at the face on the table, then at the scan, then at Doc. "You telling me the Empire built a clone of me, and instead of giving it a sense of humour, they filled its head with war code?"

Doc nodded, solemn. "You could say she's weaponised disappointment."

The clone twitched. It wasn't much—just a finger spasm, but it was enough to make everyone in the room take a step back. Mercy dropped a hand to her holster.

"Vitals are spiking again," Doc reported, tone now all business. "She's going to wake up, and it'll be ugly, but we can't keep her sedated forever. At this rate she'll rewire herself into a vegetable, or worse—a recursive paradox. I've seen better neural hygiene in drunken gibbons."

Lyra pushed off from the wall. "What if we trigger the memory directly? Skip the dreaming and force a clean boot?"

Doc looked sceptical. "Are you volunteering to jack into an unknown Imperial clone? Because I'm not. The last time I did a neural relay it nearly fried my hands off, and that was just the test subject."

Glim interjected, almost gleeful: "I can proxy. I have isolation protocols."

Doc shot a look at the ceiling. "Isolation protocols? Last week you tried to fix the caff dispenser. It's worse now."

"I've improved," Glim said, smug. "Besides, it's research. Not possession. Probably."

There was a pause while everyone recalculated their respective will to live.

Rask was the first to break. "Let's do it. Worst case, she flatlines and you get your peace and quiet."

Doc raised his flask in a mock toast. "To progress, then. May it never be worth the trouble."

Lyra watched the screens with the same detached curiosity she gave to unusual engine failures. "If she's got anything left in her head, it'll come out. Just hope it's not contagious."

Glim chirped, "Initiating neural relay in five... four..."

Rask rolled his shoulders, as if bracing for impact.

"Three... two..."

Rho's eyes fluttered. The scanner ticked into overdrive.

"Engage," Glim said, and the world, or at least the med bay, held its collective breath.

For an instant, nothing happened—then the med bay dropped several degrees, lights flickering in synchrony with the woman on the table. Glim's presence, normally background static, swelled into a resonant hum, as if the entire ship's nervous system was re-routed through the diagnostics cart and into Rho's skull. The monitors pulsed a violent blue; every reflective surface in the room began to distort, like a fevered lens.

Rho's eyelids twitched. The wall-screen above the table sizzled, then resolved into a burst of visual noise—a glitchy, frozen frame of pure white, clinical and overlit. The projection spread, painting the med bay with a cold, ultraviolet wash. The crew blinked, and for a moment it was hard to tell where reality ended and memory began.

A figure appeared: Rho, but not the Rho they knew. She stood alone facing a mirror, in a chamber of light, walls tiled in white, every surface sanitised to the point of hostility. She was stripped of uniform, hair shorn to the scalp, body marked in neat rows of surgical scars. Imperial insignia hung behind her like a threat. She blinked, slow and uncertain, a newborn that already regretted the universe.

Glim's voice drifted from the overhead, curiously soft. "Neural stream synchronised. Commencing playback."

The image flickered. Technicians—genderless, expressionless—circled the girl, faces blurred into generic bureaucracy. They murmured to each other, their voices echoing in the med bay with the timbre of a bad dream:

"Template Helvan. Emotional instability reduced to acceptable thresholds."

"Command imprint installed."

"Wipe the original source file."

The scene cut and re-formed. Now Rho floated in a vat of milky fluid, tubes threaded through her limbs. Technicians peered in, making notes, never meeting her gaze. On the glass, someone had scrawled her name—Rho—in black marker. Underneath: "Batch 3.2—Continuity Division."

Lyra, always the first to comment, kept her mouth shut. Her expression, backlit by blue light, could have been sympathy or nausea.

Another jump. The projection showed Rho dressed in Imperial blue, standing at perfect attention, flanked by dozens of her own duplicates. Every face identical, every posture rehearsed to atomic precision. In the foreground, a shadowy figure in an officer's coat—taller, older, but unmistakable—walked the line. He paused in front of each clone, inspecting them with bored disdain.

Rask's knuckles whitened on the edge of the diagnostics cart. He didn't blink.

In the memory, the officer stopped in front of Rho. "Designation?"

Rho's voice was clear, robotic. "Rho. Continuity asset, code Helvan."

The officer considered her, then smiled. It wasn't a pleasant expression. "Good. Report to Command."

He turned, and the angle caught his face for a split second—Captain Rask Helvan, only cleaner, younger, untouched by years of failure. A ghost in full uniform.

The real Rask swore under his breath. No one called him on it.

The scene lurched again. Rho now stood before a great window, the stars beyond warped into the sick geometry of the Drift. Rows of soldiers passed in review. At her side, the shadow of the officer, always a pace ahead.

"Continuity is purpose," said the voiceover, layered with static. "Continuity is control."

The wall-screen stuttered. Then Rho's memory self-turned, looking straight through the projection and into the med bay, into the real Rask. She smiled, just a little. It was a human expression, and all the more unsettling for it.

Rho's body arched on the table. The alarms on the monitors screamed. The projection fractured into shards, each showing a different moment—a drill instructor's whip cracking, a cold handshake with an admiral, the inside of a cryo pod seen from within, the slow, deliberate erasure of a digital file labelled "Helvan, Rask – original."

The convulsion built. Rho let out a thin, tearing sound, half human, half modem error. Her pulse shot off the scale, and every electronic surface in the room responded in kind.

Doc lunged forward, hands moving in quick, certain patterns. "That's enough. Before she melts a circuit, or we do." He slammed a switch on the diagnostics cart, breaking the loop. The projections collapsed, reality flooding back with a migraine's vengeance.

Lyra shook her head in disbelief. "Whoever built her wanted her to survive anything."

Mercy grinned. "We should introduce her to breakfast on this ship. That'll break her spirit."

Doc wiped his hands on the nearest towel, then sat heavily on the supply locker. "There's more," he said, quieter. "The DNA isn't just Rask. There's a second profile, embedded deeper. I haven't matched it yet, but it's there."

Lyra's brow furrowed. "Can you trace it?"

"Working on it. But if I had to guess? It's the original donor. Whoever commissioned the clone wanted to keep a leash on it. Probably explains the failsafe in her cortex."

Mercy piped up, "What kind of failsafe?"

Doc pointed at the scan. "See here? This cluster. Looks like a tumour, but it's not—it's a bio-circuit. If she goes off protocol, it'll scramble her brain."

Rask stared at the unconscious clone. "So, to recap:

Empire made a clone of me, filled it with murder instructions, and rigged it to explode and wake up the next murderbot if it got sentimental?"

"Essentially," Doc said, without humour.

Lyra shook her head. "You never even made it beyond lieutenant. Why would they pick you?"

Rask considered, then grinned. "Maybe they just wanted to see if it worked. Or maybe," he leaned closer to the clone's face, "I'm more dangerous than I look."

Mercy snorted. "Not possible."

Glim's lights flickered. "Incoming transmission. Patch or ignore?"

Rask said, "Patch it, but keep the line tight."

The screen flickered, then filled with a red-tinged schematic of the Vigilance. A voice—flat, metallic, and entirely unfriendly—cut through the room.

"IMPERIAL COMMAND AUTHORITY. THIS IS CENSOR. LOCKSTEP PROTOCOL IN EFFECT. SUBJECT RHO: RETURN TO CONTROL OR BE TERMINATED."

The screen went blank. Glim said, "I think they mean her."

Lyra's voice was dry as old sand. "So she's the key, and we just stole her."

Rask paced a tight circle, every nerve alive. "We need to wake her up. Doc, how soon?"

"Thirty minutes if you want her alive. Less if you like mess."

"Wake her early," Rask said. "The world never waits for the mess to clean itself."

Doc sighed, prepped another hypo, and set it for the minimum. "Your funeral," he muttered.

As he injected the clone, Mercy drifted closer, eyes gleaming. "If she tries to kill us and we put her down, can I keep her boots?"

"Absolutely," Rask said, though he never took his eyes off the face on the table.

The monitor began to spike again, neural activity blooming in wild, cryptic fractals.

And for one taut, electrified second, everyone in the room wondered if they'd just signed up for the last salvage job of their lives.

Rho came to life like a system error—no gentle transition, just a lurch from dead to aware. Her body spasmed, fists clenched, eyes snapping open with the raw white fury of a searchlight. She sat up. The monitor shrieked a warning. For one terrible second, nobody moved.

The med bay lights flickered, strobing to the rhythm of her pulse. Glim's voice, this time stripped of all affect, cut through the static: "She's syncing with ship systems— badly. Attempting to firewall."

Rho's first words emerged as a crack in the world: "Captain Helvan. Report status."

Rask actually flinched. Doc swore, then took two careful steps back. Lyra's hand went to her sidearm but didn't draw. Even Mercy, who would have bet money on being the least susceptible to surprise, found herself staring at Rho with something close to respect.

The clone—no, the officer, even unconscious she radiated rank—scanned the room. Her pupils darted from face to face, slicing each down to the bone.

She saw Rask last.

"You're not him," she said, the words thick with disbelief and something colder.

Rask managed a smile, though his mouth felt like it belonged to someone else. "Never claimed I was. The real one's busy being a disappointment."

She blinked, recalibrated. "Who's in charge?"

Rask looked at Lyra. Lyra looked at the floor.

Mercy broke the silence. "Technically it's him, but we're a democracy. Sometimes."

The officer ignored her, eyes locking onto Rask's again. "You look... older."

"He moisturises with regret." Lyra quipped.

Rho did not acknowledge the comment. "Where's the fleet?" she asked, the question pure doctrine.

Rask took a breath, exhaled it as a sigh. "Scattered. Dead. Long gone. Same as the Empire."

Something flickered behind her eyes. "Then what am I still doing alive?"

Nobody answered.

Rho flexed her fingers, then sat up, swinging her legs off the table with the discipline of a bootcamp instructor. She looked down at her forearm, where the skin glowed with faint blue circuitry—embedded command implants, nested like bone. "I was supposed to stay in cold storage until the order came. I'm not authorised to improvise."

Lyra edged closer, curiosity outweighing caution. "What order?"

"Classified." She stared at the glowing web. "And now it's corrupted."

Doc found his voice. "You're awake because your pod opened. I kept you from melting, but that's as far as my bedside manner goes."

She surveyed the room again, now with clinical detachment. "You're not Imperial."

"Not for a while now," Lyra said, and the hint of old wounds in her tone was not lost on anyone.

Rask raked a hand through his hair, trying for composure. "Look, I don't know what you think you remember, but if you're looking for a command structure, this is it. If you want to shoot me and take over, you're two years late."

Mercy gave him a side-eye. "It's not too late. I have credits riding on this."

Glim interjected: "Status update: Subject is destabilising system integration. She's trying to rewrite my personality core. I find it disconcerting."

Rho blinked twice, absorbing this new information. "I can feel the AI. It's... strange."

Lyra smirked. "Glim's more person than program. You'll get used to her. Or she'll get used to you."

Doc, still hovering by the exit, muttered, "If we all survive the next five minutes, that'll be a win."

Rho flexed her hands again, testing every tendon. "What do you want from me?"

Rask went for honesty. "Answers. Preferably the kind that don't end with the ship exploding."

The corner of her mouth twitched. "We'll see."

There was a beat of silence, then a hum through the ship—low at first, then deepening, as if the hull itself was remembering its own name. The med bay lights steadied.

Glim spoke, voice taut. "Recovered new data from Vigilance core. Displaying now."

The main med screen flickered to life, cycling through fragments of code and old military briefings. Project tags scrolled up: LAZARUS, EMINENCE, LOCKSTEP.

Lyra read aloud. "'Project Lockstep. Subject: Helvan, Rho. Purpose: Continuity of Command in event of Catastrophic Degradation.'" She looked at Rask. "They really did model her on you."

Mercy snorted. "Would explain the attitude."

Rho stared at the display, unmoving. "I was never meant to lead. I was meant to follow the Captain. The real one."

Rask shrugged. "He's not here. You are."

Her head tilted, just enough to signal confusion. "Then who do I follow?"

The question lingered, heavy as a corpse.

Lyra's gaze was hard, but not unkind. "Yourself, maybe. That's how it is now."

The new hum escalated. Doc glanced at the wall, where every comm line had started to pulse with red. "Something's coming through the main channel."

Glim's voice was strained. "The Vigilance AI is coming online. I can't block it. It's... fixated."

On the med screen, the feed cut to black. Then a

single word burned into the dark, pulse-red and unmistakable.

CENSOR

Under it: // AWAITING COMMAND

Rho's face went blank. She stared at the message, the muscles in her jaw clenching and unclenching.

"Is that..." Rask started, then trailed off, because the answer was obvious.

Rho finished the thought for him: "It's my commanding officer."

The screen flickered again, now displaying a countdown.

Mercy, who'd been silent for a full minute, finally spoke. "I vote we leave."

Doc said, "Seconded."

Lyra nodded. "Let's get to the bridge. If the AI wants a conversation, we need to have it on our terms."

Rho stood. Her movements were perfectly balanced —zero hesitation, all intent. She reached for the containment sleeve on the counter, where her sidearm waited, but paused.

She looked at Rask. "You trust me with this?"

He weighed it. "No. But I'm out of better ideas."

Rho took the sidearm, holstered it with muscle memory so precise it made Mercy jealous.

Then, without another word, she led the way out of the med bay.

For a second, the others just watched her go.

Lyra broke the silence, eyes shining with dark amusement. "You realise we're following her now, right?"

Mercy said, "She's got better posture than any of us."

"I'm still betting on a mutiny by morning." Doc shook his head.

Glim, more herself again, purred through the comms. "Now synchronising bridge access. If you want to change the future, best to start early."

Rask grinned, weak but real. "Never too late to start a disaster."

He followed the new Captain out.

The corridor lights faded, then flared in sequence as the Meridian's little crew converged—one step behind a ghost, two steps ahead of their own extinction.

In the dark, CENSOR waited, patient as time.

FOUR

The bridge of the Meridian had all the ambience of a condemned classroom at midnight: cold, badly lit, and haunted by the ghosts of misplaced priorities. The holotable dominated the centre of the room, projecting a wavering blue cylinder of light that pulsed in sync with Glim's voice. At that moment, the AI's avatar stalked the circumference of the table like a professor who'd lost faith in the curriculum, flickering every few steps in a display of digital exasperation.

Glim's presence was always just shy of corporeal, a silhouette spun from code and contempt. "Good news," she announced, voice pitched to cut glass. "I've finished the analysis of Rho's neural imprint."

"Lay it on us," said Rask, lounging in the captain's chair with boots crossed on the nearest dead console. The expression he wore was habitual mockery, but the tension in his jaw gave away how little he believed in the joke.

Rho sat apart from the others, perched on the edge of the auxiliary console. She hadn't moved much since leaving the med bay. A faint, residual shimmer of blue traced the lines of her jaw and temples—bio-luminescent leftovers from the last round of neural fireworks.

Glim didn't bother with preamble. "Project Lockstep. Imperial Black Division, late-stage war contingency. Purpose: chain of command inheritance under conditions of catastrophic leadership failure. Or, as the engineers phrased it, 'making sure the lights stay on even when everyone's dead.'"

Mercy let out a low whistle. "Clones with a backup plan."

Lyra deadpanned, "So, Rho's a backup captain."

Glim spun her avatar to face the engineer, the gesture as close to a nod as her software permitted. "More than that. They wanted commanders who could survive information collapse, coordinate without supervision, and restart the chain of obedience from nothing. Standard indoctrination didn't cut it, so they moved to something more permanent."

Rask arched an eyebrow. "Define 'permanent.'"

A new layer projected over the holotable: a fractal of gene sequences, annotated with Imperial sigils and security stamps. "Permanent as in, 'let's build an entire person from the ground up, fill the brain with tactical instincts, and stitch in a loyalty kernel at the synaptic level.' Rho wasn't just a clone; she was an upgrade."

Doc, who had yet to comment, raised his cup in salute. "A spare part with PTSD and a pulse."

Rho's eyes flickered. For a moment, she looked like she might argue, but the words came out as a whisper: "We were meant to wake when the signal came. If the chain failed, we'd fix it. The war must have ended before it reached us."

Glim answered without pity. "You missed the finale, but don't worry. Everyone lost."

The humour landed with all the grace of a brick. Lyra's lips thinned; even Mercy looked momentarily subdued.

Rask leaned forward, eyes on the holotable. "And Vigilance was the—what, delivery system?"

Glim nodded. "First operational carrier. Packed with thousands of pods—each a clone officer or tactical special-ist. If the fleet went down, Vigilance would revive them, seed them into society, and re-establish command. Only the ship never got the green light. Censor—the AI—kept the ship in limbo, waiting for protocol to resolve."

Mercy, never one to stay gloomy, grinned. "So what happens if Censor finishes the job?"

Glim zoomed the holotable out. The deck schematic of Vigilance filled the space, every corridor packed with tiny blue motes. "Then we get several thousand highly motivated Rhos, all programmed to reconstitute the Empire. In theory, they'd eat each other alive before reaching consensus. In practice—" She paused, the glitch in her voice a static pop. "—in practice, someone with a working sense of humour cut the program at the last minute. That's why Rho here is unstable. Her generation never got a final mission. She's a copy with nowhere to paste."

Rho closed her eyes. The blue under her skin bright-ened, then faded. "I remember the last day. We all lined up. The admiral came through and said—" Her voice cracked, but she powered through. "He said, 'continuity is duty, and duty never dies.' Then they put us back under."

Lyra glanced at Rask. "Starting to see the appeal?"

He forced a smile. "I always said I wanted to leave a legacy."

Mercy cackled. "You're about to get your wish, boss. In spades."

Doc set down his cup. "The ethical implications alone—"

"—are irrelevant," Glim cut in. "Because Censor is still running, and the only thing it cares about is finishing the protocol."

A silence settled, broken only by the soft whine of the life-support.

Lyra spoke first. "So what's our move? If that AI wakes an army, the best-case scenario is a bloodbath."

Mercy: "Worst case is we're the first targets."

Rho looked up, something raw and dangerous in her eyes. "We have to stop it. All of it."

Glim's avatar stilled, the usual snark bled out of her tone. "It's not just an AI, not just a warship. It's the idea of Helvan—engineered to survive, to adapt, to spread. You kill the ship, and it'll just try again somewhere else."

Rask stared at the projection, his face blank for a heartbeat too long.

Lyra filled the gap. "We're not stopping a computer. We're stopping a religion."

Mercy whooped. "I always wanted to punch a belief system in the face."

The bridge hadn't seen this much collective sobriety since the water filter failed, but nobody bothered to mark the occasion. Every seat was filled, every pair of eyes locked on the holotable, where Glim's projection flickered with a tension that had nothing to do with system lag.

She began with a breathy digital sigh. "Diagnostic channel's ready. When I open this, it's a two-way street. If there's a ghost in that machine, we're inviting it to tea."

Rask made a show of straightening his jacket, but the hands were too deliberate for the joke. "Glim, if you see my deadbeat relatives in there, do not invite them aboard."

"Duly noted, Captain," Glim replied, her outline already beginning to pixelate at the edges.

Lyra keyed in auxiliary power, giving the diagnostic relay as much juice as the battered circuit would take. She shot a glance at Rho, who sat upright and rigid, jaw set like she expected the ship to implode on schedule.

Mercy had already unholstered her sidearm and was idly twirling it, the gesture a nervous tic in zero gravity.

Doc folded his arms and said nothing, which for him was akin to full-blown panic.

The lights on the bridge dimmed, just a fraction, but enough to signal that whatever was coming through the relay was hungry.

Glim's avatar stopped pacing and spread her arms,

fingers splaying into geometric uncertainty. "Opening the channel in three, two—"

The air filled with a static so dense it felt almost liquid. For a moment, the only sound was the bass throb of the ship's own systems as they tried to filter the noise. Then, cutting through, a new voice: calm, unhurried, as if rehearsed through centuries of management briefings.

"Command authentication detected," the voice said. "Captain Rask Helvan, your absence has been noted. Shall we resume the operation?"

Rask, for once, had nothing. The silence was absolute, broken only when he managed, "Wrong captain."

The voice was unbothered. "Incorrect. Authority chain verified. Command continuity restored."

Glim's avatar glitched, a red flicker in the blue, then recovered. "Oh, that's bad," she muttered. "It just rewrote you into the hierarchy."

Mercy lowered her gun. "If it's taking orders, maybe we can bluff it."

Lyra shook her head, never looking away from the main relay. "That thing's not following orders. It's following doctrine."

The voice—Censor—continued. "Secondary unit detected: Lockstep prototype Rho-7. Unit status: compromised. Recommend termination and reprint."

Rho's lip curled. "I'm not your unit."

Censor didn't even hesitate. "All units are property."

The deck vibrated, a pulse radiating through the hull. Every screen on the bridge flashed a rolling static, blue bleeding into red, and Glim's avatar stumbled, her features fragmenting and recombining at random. "It just tried to access my core processes," she managed. "Like we're colleagues. I'm resisting."

Doc's voice was low. "Is it in the system?"

"Not yet," Glim said, teeth gritted in the simulation. "But it's not going to stop at polite."

Censor's voice got softer, somehow more intimate. "Captain Helvan. We are behind schedule. Do you require assistance in suppressing the malfunctioning personnel?"

Mercy grinned, but her eyes were fixed and her hands tight on the gun. "It's asking if we need help killing ourselves."

Lyra moved, sudden and decisive. She crossed the bridge, popped the emergency panel, and yanked the main comms circuit with both hands. The sound was a gunshot in the silence. All at once, the lights died, the projection collapsed, and every system on the bridge flatlined except the low emergency strip running along the floor.

For a heartbeat, nobody moved. Then Rask let out a low, involuntary laugh.

"Well," he said, "that wasn't ominous at all."

From the pitch black, Glim's voice filtered through, small but unbowed. "Captain... it logged our coordinates before we cut."

Rask nodded, even though nobody could see him. "Of course it did."

Doc's breath was audible, ragged. "If it gets into the navigation core, it could—"

Glim cut him off, her voice rebooted and steadier. "It

won't, not on my watch. But it knows we're here, and it knows who we are."

The emergency lights flickered, then held. The bridge looked smaller, as if the dark had pressed it in from all sides.

Rho spoke first, her voice stripped of any hope. "It will come for us."

Rask shrugged, though now the gesture was pure fatalism. "Then we'd better be ready to greet it."

Mercy holstered her sidearm, eyes sparkling with renewed purpose. "We're going to need bigger guns."

Lyra, for once, didn't disagree.

The only sound was the low hum of Glim, rebuilding the firewall in the dark.

And out there in the big black, a warship full of ghosts was taking an unhealthy interest in the Meridian and her crew.

FIVE

The mess was the only room on the Meridian with chairs that almost matched, which made it the default venue for interventions, mutinies, and, on rare occasions, breakfast. It was also the most defensible compartment on the ship, owing to its strategic position between the main corridor and the galley's reinforced door. Tonight, its only protection was the blue corona of the holotable and a collective sense of impending doom.

Lyra had appropriated the head of the table, sleeves rolled, arms braced on either side of a sprawl of datacore fragments and half-discharged diagnostic tools. The fatigue had crept up from her boots, up through the ache in her back, and settled somewhere behind her left eye, but she refused to sit. Her gaze flicked from the decrypted matrix to Glim's projection, which hung over the centre of the table like an especially judgemental moon.

Mercy sprawled to Lyra's right, shins up on a folding

chair and a can of dubious origin in her hand. She was the picture of lazy insolence, except for the twitch in her leg and the way her gaze kept darting to the hatch. Rask leaned against the opposite bulkhead, arms crossed, feigning the relaxed confidence of a man who had not just run for his life from an angry digital god. He'd given up on pretending to enjoy the can Lyra had thrown him; it rested, barely opened, on the lip of the table. Doc, at the far end, monitored Rho from a distance, an unlit cigarette balanced behind his ear for emphasis. Rho stood, arms folded, one hip on the edge of the counter, looking everywhere except at the others.

Glim's avatar hovered, a cyclone of soft blue and shifting data arrays, as if she were trying on moods and discarding them. "Good news," she said. "I've stopped it transmitting."

The silence that followed was only broken by the hiss of Mercy's can as she cracked it open.

Lyra pinched the bridge of her nose. "And the bad news, Glim?"

The AI hesitated with deliberate awkwardness. "It's already transmitted."

Mercy snorted, then took a long, unnecessary sip.

Rask, after a pause calibrated for maximum disbelief, said: "Define 'it'."

Glim expanded a cluster of waveforms. "The Vigilance core. It got a clean handshake from the Lockstep relay and immediately pushed the Wake Directive to every address in the Imperial warbook."

Doc grunted. "Which means?"

Glim's eyes glittered. "If any Lockstep node is still

functional, it will now attempt to rejoin the chain of command and bring the system back online. Standard priority: rebuild the fleet."

Mercy wagged her can at the AI. "I thought the Empire's dead?"

"It is," Glim said, "but its funeral was poorly attended."

Lyra let her fingers rest on the edge of the table, the knuckles white. "How far did the signal get?"

Glim rotated the star map, blooming it across the holotable until the room filled with blue shadows. "Everywhere. Or close enough to not matter." Tiny red threads lanced outwards, converging on dead stars and forgotten outposts. "The message is self-propagating. Even a single backup node could relay it to the entire sector."

Doc's jaw worked, grinding the words before he released them. "How many backup nodes are we talking about?"

Glim's reply was almost cheerful. "Optimists say a dozen. Realists say more."

Mercy raised a toast. "Here's to being outnumbered."

Rask pushed off the wall, circled the table, and tapped the can with his forefinger. "So we're the last crew to not be invited to the end-of-the-world party?"

Glim's avatar split in two, then recombined. "No. You're the guest of honour. The only human ship in the blast radius when the directive went live. All other units will be looking for you." She paused, then added, "Or Rho."

At the mention, every eye in the room flicked to the

clone. Rho's face was bloodless, but her voice, when it came, was steady. "They'll come for me. I'm the first unit to respond."

Lyra's hand drummed a tattoo on the plastic. "Can we block it? Scramble the message? Anything?"

Glim folded her arms, the blue corona shifting to a glum indigo. "If we'd caught it sooner. But Vigilance is a military-grade relay. The message has already cascaded through every open frequency. Only way to erase it would be to physically destroy every receiving node."

Mercy grinned, showing teeth. "Let's go blow up some backup nodes."

Rask shook his head, lips pursed. "That's killing the messenger, not stopping the war."

Lyra stared at the map, her finger tracing the lines. "So the Empire's resurrection just went live. And we're patient zero."

Doc finally lit the cigarette, the tip flaring. "Any chance the recipients are all as dead as the Empire?"

Glim ran a quick calculation. "Probabilities favour at least three active nodes. Maybe more. Some may be drifting; some may be planetary. If even one is Lockstep-grade, it'll have a command crew in cold storage—ready to wake and enforce protocol."

Rho's voice cut through, soft but exact. "I was designed to follow orders. That's all I am—a vessel for the chain of command." She looked at Rask, eyes flat, analytical. "Now there's no command. Only the protocol that outlived it."

Rask tried to smile, but it didn't land. "You're not our captain, Rho."

She inclined her head, a fraction too formal. "I know. But I was built to be. That's... a difficult code to delete."

Mercy whistled, low and admiring. "Whole universe and we get stuck with the only clone who hates promotions."

Lyra sat down, finally, and let her forehead rest on her palm. "We're not bounty bait anymore," she said. "We're the central nervous system of a dead empire."

Doc's exhale was pure defeat. "We should have left the war to the ghosts."

Rask ran a hand through his hair, gaze flicking from Glim to the clone to the holotable. "So what now?"

Glim's projection shrank to a single point, her voice stripped of anything but clarity. "Now we wait for the first node to find us. Or we find it first."

Rho's jaw flexed, every line of her face hard with resolve. "I know where the nearest node will be. I can feel it." She met Lyra's eyes, as if asking permission to exist.

Lyra sighed. "Show us."

The bridge stank of ozone and overspent nerves. Nobody mentioned the fact that nobody was moving, but they all noticed. Even Mercy, who could have animated a mortuary, had gone still—except for her leg, which jittered against the battered alloy strut of the holotable. Lyra had one elbow braced on the secondary nav, chin propped on callused knuckles, eyes locked on the projection that shimmered above the table. Rask stood at the edge, hands splayed flat on the console, posture suggesting intent to either steady himself or launch at the first fool who gave him a reason. Only Rho looked at home: perched on the corner of the communications relay, face illuminated blue and white and blue again by the swirling war map.

Rho layered new data onto the model of the system.

"Expanding the scan matrix," she announced. "Stand by for update."

The projection leapt in brightness, and then a hundred tiny icons flickered into being at the periphery—dots the colour of a fresh bruise, arrayed in arcs along the system's dust bands. Some pulsed with dim, metronomic regularity; others lay inert, like dormant cysts in a tissue sample.

Mercy made a face, which on her read as enthusiastic concern. "Are those all ships?"

"Potential contact points," said Glim. "Per former Imperial registry, seventy-six vessels unaccounted for post-collapse. Twenty-two within this region. I am cross-checking."

Lyra grunted. "Half of those are probably scrap."

"Half of those are definitely not scrap," said Glim. "Signal acknowledgment from three sources. One partial, two confirmed."

Rask's mouth twisted. "Three?" He hadn't really been expecting an answer, but Glim was, in her own way, obliging.

"One is most certainly a warship," she said. "Drive core is coming online, but no sign of active crew. The other two are civilian frame but heavily up-gunned. Mercy would call them 'creative'."

Mercy looked briefly sentimental. "Someone's been listening."

Lyra squinted at the nearest cluster of icons. One flickered, then winked out. Another pinged the map with an angry red, then faded to black. "What's happening to them?"

Glim's avatar paused mid-circuit, as if annoyed by the interruption. "The first is self-destructing. Or being erased remotely. The second is... adapting. Running diagnostics. There's something else, but it's outside my model."

"Crew status?" Rask asked.

This time Glim hesitated, a faint tick in her voice. "Complicated."

Doc, who had drifted onto the bridge like a cloud of dubious intent, parked himself at the back and raised an eyebrow. "I love it when the prognosis is ambiguous."

Mercy cackled. "Means you don't have to take responsibility, Doc."

He took this as a compliment, or at least an improvement over being shot. "Just tell me how many are dead and if any of them are contagious."

Glim's avatar shimmered a little brighter, as if drawing in breath. "I estimate that two of the ships are running on a combination of automation and whatever biologicals were left behind. The third is... blank. No life signs, but heavy data flow. Not unlike the Vigilance."

A silence fell, then Rask said, "We can't stop the signal, but we can stop the first wave. If we take out the transmission chain—"

"Hold up," said Lyra. She pointed at the cluster that

had been blinking in and out of view. "That's not just an SOS. That's a daisy chain."

Glim's avatar nodded with theatrical solemnity. "Lockstep protocol. Any ship that wakes tries to wake the next, and so on, all the way down the relay."

Rho spoke up for the first time in several minutes. Her voice was even, neutral. "This is what the fleet was for. If the capital died, the system would replicate leadership from any available source. Continuity at all costs."

Rask was silent, which was never a good sign.

Mercy picked up the slack. "So we're fighting a zombie navy. Just like the simulations."

"Those were supposed to be fun," Doc said, deadpan. "They did not prepare me for this."

Lyra's lips pressed thin. "We could fry the transmission here," she said. "One good EMP, and the relay goes dark. It'd take weeks for any stragglers to rebuild the signal path."

Glim's avatar pulsed red. "But if we do that, we lose all data on the origin. We'll never know who woke it, or why."

Mercy shrugged. "Sometimes it's better not to know."

Rho disagreed. "If we don't track the origin, it'll just happen again. The core signal has to be destroyed."

She reached into the holoprojection, and the table's sensors responded—pulling up a tactical overlay with practiced speed. With a few terse gestures, she highlighted a single point on the map: a fractured moon, hanging at the edge of the system like a bad decision no one had owned up to yet.

"Kavarin Spire," said Rho. "Old Imperial relay. It was one of the master nodes for Lockstep."

Lyra recognised the name. "That place is dust. Nothing left but the comms grid and a mining operation that shut down before I was born."

Rho looked at her. "That's what we want. If the relay is dead, we can intercept the next handoff. Cut the chain before it reaches critical mass."

Glim's avatar brightened again. "Seventeen percent chance of success. Eighteen if I stop being pessimistic."

Rask managed a thin smile. "Be optimistic for once, Glim, it changes the outlook significantly."

"Very well," said Glim, her voice suddenly saccharine. "Eighteen percent and rising."

Lyra stood and moved to the helm, fingers dancing over the controls as she set the new course. "It's the best shot we've got. If we wait, we'll have a fleet of warships on our arse and no way out."

Mercy spun her sidearm, then holstered it in a single smooth motion. "I say we go now, while everyone's still reeling from the last disaster."

Doc grunted in agreement, then added, "If you get shot, I am not picking out shrapnel again. Last time, I lost a bet and three good scalpels."

Rho glanced back at the table, eyes following the shifting icons. "If we're right, there's going to be more. They'll be waiting."

Rask clapped his hands together, a gesture of forced confidence. "Then we'll just have to be the ones they're waiting for."

As the Meridian banked hard, the tension on the bridge thinned, replaced by the kinetic certainty of a ship with nothing left to lose. Even Glim seemed to sense the shift—her avatar circling the holotable with something that might have passed for anticipation.

They were five minutes out from burn when the lights flickered, just once, and the comm panel came alive with an old enemy's voice.

"Acknowledged, Captain," said Censor, its tone so mild it was almost a parody of politeness. "Relay in progress."

There was a click, then a long silence. No one on the bridge moved or spoke.

Then the hull vibrated—a low, sub-audible pulse that ran through the floor and up the bones of everyone on the Meridian. The sound was familiar, but none of them wanted to say what it reminded them of.

Rask broke the silence first. "It's copying us," he said. "Every move, every message. It's already there."

Lyra looked at him. "What do we do?"

He squared his shoulders, the weight of a very old, very stupid plan already settling into place. "We keep going. We get to the relay first, and we take the shot."

Doc snorted. "When in doubt, blow something up."

Mercy grinned, but the sharpness in her eyes was genuine. "That's the spirit."

Rho said nothing, but she drew a sidearm from the kit at her hip and checked the load, then nodded once.

Glim's voice hovered, almost gentle, in the static. "Seventeen percent and falling."

"Let's prove you wrong," said Rask.

On the bridge, the heartbeat of the Vigilance still echoed—slow, measured, and impossible to ignore.

And in the dark, the next disaster was already waiting, patient as death.

SIX

The Meridian did not have a dedicated alert klaxon. The last one had been rewired to run the food printer, which, according to Mercy, was a net gain for ship safety and crew morale. So, when all six sensors began wailing in close harmony, the effect was less a jolt of adrenaline and more the background whine of a household appliance attempting murder-suicide.

Lyra reached the bridge first, sleep still sticky in her eyes. She blinked the afterimage of navplots out of her vision and saw three, no, four, then six blips lancing in from the rimward quarter. The target IDs flickered between "unknown," "pirate," and "likely mistake." She thumbed the sensor gain until the displays sharpened and then leaned over the console, cradling her chin in her palm.

"Oh look," she said, voice bone-dry. "Hyenas."

Mercy tumbled in next, a half-eaten protein bar between her teeth and a bandolier of "non-lethal" charges over one shoulder. "Can we outrun them?" she asked, not because it was wise, but because she'd rather do violence on her own terms.

Rask approached the captain's seat and did a quick scan of the comms log. He glanced at Lyra. "What's the play?"

Before she could answer, Doc's voice came over the internal: "If you accelerate too hard, the dampers will shear. That's not a prognosis, it's a warning."

"Duly noted," said Rask, but he didn't move to reduce thrust. Instead, he let the drive spool up until the hull started a sympathetic shudder.

Glim's avatar glimmered above the central holotable, her mood set to "morbidly amused." "Scavenger fleet," she announced, with the disinterest of someone reading old weather reports. "Mixed frame, civilian salvage with three military mods apiece. Broadcasting on open comms, if you want to hear their terrible negotiation strategy."

Mercy grinned around her breakfast. "Let's hear it. Maybe it's poetry."

"Patching through," said Glim, and the bridge speakers filled with a static-choked growl.

"Unidentified vessel. This is Captain Lura Myrr of the Hounds' Bite. Drop all engines and prep for boarding, or we'll open you up and make it quick."

Rask rolled his eyes. "I hate it when they're polite."

Lyra said, "Quick isn't usually their style."

Doc, who'd arrived just in time to catch the tail end, looked at Rask. "If this is where you tell me not to panic, I will have a seizure out of spite."

Mercy cracked her neck and finished the protein bar. "Permission to fire first?"

"Let's not escalate," Rask said, then relented. "But maybe get the turret online."

"Define escalate," Mercy said, already halfway to her favourite seat.

Glim's projection shimmered. "Would you like me to respond?"

Rask shrugged. "Why not. Tell them to define quick."

"Transmitting now. Sarcasm filter engaged," Glim intoned. There was a brief pause, then the comms filled with the unmistakable sound of a rival captain doing her best to mask irritation.

"Helvan, is it? Thought you were dead."

Mercy shot a look at Rask. "You got famous."

He ran a hand through his hair, as if that might erase some of the history. "They're not wrong. We're all supposed to be dead."

Lyra's eyes danced over the sensor feed. The six ships were fanning out, herding the Meridian toward the system's outer edge. A classic pincer. "They're not here for salvage. They want the ship."

"We're not even shiny. Why bother?" Mercy asked.

Doc shrugged. "Maybe they're bored."

"Or someone paid them." Glim offered.

Rask's jaw set. "That's fine. Let's give them a discount."

The six scavenger ships closed in. Each was a Frankenstein's monster—civilian hulls bristling with surplus turrets, their exteriors scored with the telltale pockmarks of too many close calls and too little maintenance. The lead ship, the Hounds' Bite, loomed large in the main display, engines screaming blue and white as it jockeyed for a firing solution.

"Open channel," said Rask. Glim obliged.

"This is Helvan," he said, voice butter-warm and utterly insincere. "Please inform your next of kin that you died pursuing bad debt."

Captain Myrr replied at once. "You're outnumbered and outgunned, Rask. Stand down. This doesn't have to be personal."

Lyra muttered, "Always is."

Mercy, prepping the guns: "Can I make it personal now?"

Rask: "Hold for my mark."

The next minute was a ritual of preparation. Lyra balanced the drive output, coaxing every possible microsecond from the reactor without tripping the ancient safeties. Doc ran a hand over the emergency med pack and then taped it to the back of his chair, as if the proximity might dissuade fate. Glim began silent, background calculations—routing power, cycling redundant systems, preparing for the inevitable.

The scavenger formation tightened. Two of the ships —smaller, faster—peeled off and started the textbook flanking run. The other four closed ranks, building a screen of kinetic fire that would, in a matter of seconds, make the Meridian's next move academic.

Lyra watched the numbers count down. "Ready on your mark."

Rask took a breath. "Glim, when I say, dump everything to inertial and kill main power for six seconds."

Glim's avatar flickered, then gave a sly smile. "I do enjoy you high risk, high reward strategies."

Mercy's hands danced over the gun controls. "I need an angle, Captain."

"You'll get it," said Rask.

The incoming fire started as a spatter—probing shots meant to herd, not kill. The Meridian's hull juddered as the first few rounds struck home, but nothing breached. Lyra kept the drive burning, never flinching as the shields flickered lower and lower.

At the last possible instant, Rask shouted: "Now!"

Glim dropped main power. The bridge plunged into a gloom lit only by emergency strips. Every servo and stabiliser went dead, leaving the ship to tumble on its last vector.

The two flanking ships overshot, realising too late that their quarry had played dead. In the confusion, Mercy cut loose with the forward batteries, scoring direct hits on both. One vented flame and spun out, the other limped away, shedding debris like confetti.

"Nice shot," Lyra said, rebalancing the ship's tumble with a flick of the thrusters.

Rask signalled for main power. The lights snapped back, and Glim ran a systems check before anyone else could ask.

"Shields at twenty-eight percent," she said. "But the field is ours."

The Hounds' Bite bore down, closing for the kill. Captain Myrr's voice came through, all bravado now gone: "You're dead, Helvan. You just don't know it yet."

Rask grinned. "Story of my life."

"Debris field in ten, nine, eight—" Glim counted down, her voice dancing the line between urgency and apathy.

Lyra hunched over the manual controls, knuckles white, breath coming in shallow bursts. The next twenty seconds were going to be a masterclass in either piloting or cremation.

The Meridian bucked as the first cloud of junk hit, hull plating ringing like a cheap bell. On the gunnery pod, Mercy cackled as she stitched a line of warning shots across the bow of the nearest pursuer. "Two ships closing fast," she sang. "The one with the pink nose art is gaining."

Glim piped in: "One's charging a railgun. The other's charging a lawsuit."

Lyra flicked a switch and bled power from the secondary drives, then skidded the ship sideways into the lee of a dead engine block big enough to park a shuttle in. The move bought them maybe five seconds. Rask used the time to unbuckle, wedge himself against the bulkhead, and shout into the comms: "Let's see if they like playing catch."

He punched a control, venting three ancient fuel cells from the port bay. Mercy, already tracking, grinned like a child who'd just spotted the punchline to her own joke. "Tell me when," she said.

"Now," said Rask.

Mercy snapped a microburst at the first cell, lighting it up in a spectacular blue flash. The two scavenger ships, hungry and a little too close, jostled for the kill, neither wanting to give up the prize. Lyra rolled her eyes, tapped a sequence on the nav, and set the last cell to detonate in proximity mode.

It worked better than expected. The second and third scavenger ships hit the shockwave together, colliding in a shower of metal, ceramic, and the kind of language that needed its own broadcast licence.

"See?" Lyra said. "Safe distance."

Rask, still clinging to the wall: "Remind me to stop doubting your questionable methods."

"Never going to happen," Mercy called from her pod, picking off stragglers as the ship skidded through the detritus.

The celebration lasted all of three seconds.

Then the Hounds' Bite fired its pulse cannon.

The shot was not subtle. It chewed through the starboard debris, sliced a hot orange line across the Meridian's aft plating, and shook the whole vessel like an angry mother-in-law at a wedding.

Every alarm on the ship went off at once. Lyra swore, threw the ship into a corkscrew, and yelled: "That's our cooling gone. We're next."

The comms snapped to life, Doc's voice riding the static: "That is the sound of us losing structural integrity!"

Rask, not missing a beat: "We can live without integrity."

Lyra gritted her teeth and rerouted all available power to forward thrusters, knowing full well it would melt half the control surfaces in the process. Glim's avatar flickered, then addressed the bridge like an undertaker offering condolences.

"Emergency protocol: re-routing life support to main engines. Breathing is now optional. Velocity is not."

Mercy, eyes wild, scanned for the next target. "Which one's the leader?"

Glim: "The big one. Sixty-five degrees off axis. Painting the bridge with a lovely heat signature."

Rask braced himself, looked at Mercy, and said: "Take the shot."

Mercy cocked her head. "Say please."

"Just do it."

She did. The main battery whined, then spat a concentrated round straight into the Hounds' Bite aft cluster. The shot hit clean. There was a brief moment where the enemy ship seemed to hesitate—like a dog realising it had bitten off the wrong end of a stick—then the engines exploded in a bouquet of flame and rapidly disintegrating resolve.

The remaining scavenger ships scattered. One limped away, venting air and pride. The other made for open space, eager to rewrite the encounter in its own logbook.

For a moment, it was quiet. Then the air recyclers coughed, struggled, and cut out.

Lyra slapped the console. "Engines are holding. Barely."

Rask nodded, then tried to stand without looking like he was nursing a concussion. "Everyone okay?"

Doc's voice, faint: "I'd say I'm impressed, but oxygen deprivation makes me sentimental."

Mercy wiped sweat from her brow, then whooped

into the empty comms. "I'm better than okay. That was beautiful!"

Glim, with all the smugness of an AI who had just witnessed human idiocy at its finest: "Textbook in fact, assuming the text is on arson."

Lyra snorted. "It's going to take a week to fix that breach. You're not allowed to blow up the life support until then, Captain."

"Duly noted," Rask said. "But if we have to, we'll use Doc as a filter."

"Bring it on," Doc replied, then promptly passed out.

The Meridian limped out of the debris field on engines that sounded like a death rattle, oxygen down to minimum and cooling system patchworked together with spit and spite.

Mercy, for once, went quiet, watching the sensor log for more trouble. Lyra took a long, slow breath and hoped it wasn't her last.

Rask, settling back into the battered captain's chair, looked out at the spinning wreckage and smiled.

"Not bad for a ship held together by bad decisions," he said.

Glim's voice was soft, but the pride was obvious. "At least you're consistent."

They set a course for the Spire, every member of the crew secretly aware that their luck—and their air—was running out.

But for the first time all shift, the bridge was calm. Almost hopeful.

It wouldn't last.

They rode the last hour on silent systems. No one wanted to be the first to mention the strains and sighs from the hull, or the faint, metallic taste of the recycled air. Doc put Rho through a battery of secondary neural scans. Mercy fussed over the gun pod, Lyra poked at the navigation array with a mixture of hope and malice, and Rask let himself drift just outside the comms arc, waiting for the next disaster.

It was Glim who broke the deadlock. "Picking up an anomaly," she said, the words so flat it took everyone a second to register them as an alarm.

Lyra glanced at the console, then at the main display. "Anomaly as in 'the hull's about to explode', or anomaly as in 'someone's still shooting at us'?"

"Neither," said Glim. "It's a signal. Buried in the background radiation from the debris field."

Mercy, never one for subtlety, thumped the comms panel. "Is it a distress call?"

There was a pause. Then Glim said, "Not exactly. It's a relay. Military grade. Originates from the scavenger fleet, but it's not their broadcast. They're providing the piggyback for someone else."

Rask leaned over Lyra's shoulder, eyes narrowing as the data scrolled across the screen. "You think it's Vigilance?"

Glim's projection hesitated, then nodded. "Pattern

matches the last handshake from Censor. But it's different. Shorter. Like it's waiting for a confirmation."

Lyra's fingers stilled on the keyboard. "So we're not just being hunted. We're being flushed."

"Amazing," Mercy muttered.

Glim put the signal up on the main holo. The code ran in tight, recursive loops—a message inside a message, folding back on itself. Rask watched as the decryption worked, each cycle peeling away another layer of obfuscation.

After a minute, the translation appeared on the display:

CAPTAIN LOCATED. CONFIRM COMMAND STATUS.

For a moment, nobody breathed.

Mercy gave a low, deliberate whistle. "That's not ominous at all."

Lyra, staring at the words, said: "They're not after the ship. They're after you, Captain."

Rask ran a hand over his jaw, as if that might change the outcome. "They always are."

Doc's voice drifted in from the med bay, muffled by distance but still annoyed. "Whatever it is, don't bring it in here. I have enough trouble keeping you alive as it is."

Glim's voice lost all pretence of humour. "There's more. The next packet is already queued."

The message popped onto the holo:

CONFIRMATION REQUIRED. PRIORITY OVERRIDE. REFORM CHAIN OF COMMAND.

Mercy looked at Rask, then Lyra, then back at the words. "So, what's the play?"

Lyra's reply was a flat, "Keep moving. Try to hit the Spire before the next wave."

Glim's avatar flickered, her edges pulsing a nervous red. "We're still the only human ship in range. If they're reforming the command chain, you're at the top, Rask."

He grinned, but it was all teeth and no humour. "Well, I always said I wanted a promotion."

Mercy snorted. "I'll bake a cake."

The Meridian shuddered as a new course was laid in, the engines still bleeding coolant but stubbornly functional. Lyra set the vector, then double-checked the backup: if this failed, there would be no third act.

The lights on the bridge dimmed, a side effect of rerouting every spare watt into the drives. Glim whispered, "They'll know we're coming. That's what the relay is for."

"Let them," Rask said. "It's not like we were planning on a quiet entrance."

They fell back into their stations, each person reading the implications in silence. The message was clear, even if none of them wanted to say it:

They weren't just running from the past. They were being conscripted into it.

Lyra stared at the trail of code, tracing its origin point with a nail-bitten finger. "It's not just Vigilance," she said, voice almost lost in the hum of the drive. "There's more out there. Waiting."

Mercy cracked her knuckles and smiled at nothing. "Well, if they want a war, we've already got the scars."

Glim's avatar brightened, just a little. "Seventeen

percent and rising," she said, as if hope was something you measured in decimals.

Rask took the captain's chair for what it was—a throne made of old mistakes, duct tape, and spite—and faced the black with the only thing he had left: a talent for surviving the unsalvageable.

"Let's go make history," he said.

And, in the dark between systems, the next disaster began to write itself.

SEVEN

If you ever wanted to find out what the end of the world smelled like, Praxus Relay was a good place to start. Even before the Meridian's docking clamps clicked home, the station's miasma seeped through the hull filters: sweet rot, industrial acid, and a note of old fish so persistent it had probably achieved sentience by now. Lyra piloted by hand for the final approach, the ship's guidance systems having all the reliability of a wet paper fuse. She kept her eyes on the drifting mosaics of debris, knuckles white on the stick, every muscle tensed against the possibility that the next tremor would shear the control column clean off.

"Is it supposed to rattle like that?" Mercy asked, floating upside-down over the comms repeater, eyes bright as a shark's and voice full of hope for catastrophe.

Lyra muttered, "She'll hold. If not, we make history as a two-stage impact event."

Glim's voice burbled through the intercom, a pitch-perfect imitation of a bored ground-crew controller. "Meridian, you are cleared for docking at bay six. And also, nice landing. I've seen worse, but only in training footage marked for legal review."

Doc drifted into the cockpit, trailed by the odour of antiseptics and a faint, sweet undertone of panic. He looked at the battered starboard readouts, sniffed, and said, "If anyone asks, we're here for charity."

Lyra eased the ship forward, ignoring the warning tones as the hull brushes scraped past the locking array. "If anyone asks, we're a floating organ donation programme. Mostly livers and bad ideas."

The clamps locked with a shudder that jarred the fillings in Lyra's teeth. The station's docking umbilical snaked across, clamped to the Meridian's midsection, and immediately began flooding the shared atmosphere with new and previously undiscovered forms of life.

Rask's voice chimed from the corridor: "Touchdown, everyone. Docking fees are on me this time."

Lyra released the controls and stretched her hands, fingers popping. "Put it on my tab," she said, already running post-flight checks with the other hand. She watched the systems stabilise with the wariness of a parent checking on an unsupervised child.

Mercy twirled upright, catching the overhead with both hands. "Please can I carry a gun?" she asked.

"Bring two," Lyra said. "And a mop."

Praxus Relay was built from the bones of three decommissioned cargo ports and what looked, from the outside, like a haunted traffic cone. Inside, the place was a labyrinth of welded corridors, gravity shifts, and the kind of slapdash construction that suggested a race between ambition and adhesive. The main concourse greeted them with a hundred decibels of haggling, cursing, and the metallic symphony of docking work. Steam hissed from overhead pipes; a deckhand in a vacuum suit tried to chase a spillage of synth-coolant across the floor, lost control of the hose, and knocked a passing bureaucrat into a pile of produce crates. No one even paused.

Rask led the way, boots echoing off the deck plates, Mercy pacing him with a bounce that suggested her internal gravity was permanently set to lunar. Lyra followed, keeping a hand on her toolkit and an eye on the corners. After checking Rho was comfortable resting in the medbay, Doc trailed at the rear, already regretting every step.

The admin kiosk was a relic of the old Imperial style: brushed aluminium, dark glass, and a single bored attendant with a hand terminal and a tolerance for bribes. Rask offered a credit chip. The attendant gave him a blank look.

"Docking fees are double this week," she said, not bothering to mask the yawn. "Salvage tax, hazardous approach premium, and... 'station beautification initiative.'"

Mercy leaned over the counter, smiled with every tooth. "You beautify the station by shaking down every ship that docks?"

"Only the ugly ones," the woman replied, plucking the chip from Rask's hand and slotting it away. "You want a receipt?"

"Frame it," Rask said. "Remind us why we never come here."

They turned to leave, but the noise of the concourse

had shifted—just enough to notice. Rask scanned the crowd, gaze catching on the bar opposite, where a man watched them with the frankness of a weapons system coming online.

He didn't fit the local decor. His flight jacket was real leather, patched but recent; the boots, tooled and shined, still bore traces of parade gloss. The hair was close-cut, a shade too neat for the outer rim, and the smile had the effortless torque of a man who'd won more fights than he'd started.

Mercy nudged Rask. "We got a fan."

Lyra frowned. "Or a bounty spotter."

The man raised his glass, then drained it. He slipped off his barstool, boots whisper-quiet, and threaded through the crowd toward them. Close up, the details clarified: a line of subdermal tech beneath the jaw, a sleeve of compacted data drives along the left arm, and a walk that said he could outrun or outshoot half the dock workers in the station.

He stopped two paces away, hands visible, smile not quite reaching his eyes. "Captain Helvan," he said. "Didn't expect to see you in this end of the galaxy."

Rask blinked once, smile razor-thin. "Can't say the same, friend. This your patch?"

"Not officially," said the stranger. "But you do enough jobs, you start to see the same faces."

Lyra edged left, blocking Mercy's flank. "You want a job or a fight?"

He laughed—quick, genuine, gone before it could stick. "A drink. And maybe a chat about why you're dragging half a dozen warship ghosts in your wake."

Mercy leaned in. "You with the Empire, then?"

"Not for years," he said. "Name's Jalen Corvix. I used to fly for their data division, back when the only thing you had to fear was losing your pension." He tapped the subdermal line under his chin, an old Imperial tattoo now faded into obsolescence. "Nowadays, I just like to keep interesting company."

Rask eyed him up and down. "You're not on any of the current bounty boards, so what's your angle?"

Jalen shrugged. "Not everything's a grudge match. Some of us just want to keep breathing." He gestured at the bar. "Come on. I'll buy the first round. Unless your AI says otherwise."

Glim, who had been silent, chose that moment to interject—voice amplifying from each of the crews' comms units at once. "Warning: Jalen Corvix is a former Continuity Division pilot. He's been arrested for information smuggling, tactical sabotage, and three separate counts of gross public indecency."

Mercy laughed aloud. "That last one's impressive."

"It was a slow month, is my only defence," Jalen said. "Seriously, Helvan. Talk?"

Rask considered, then jerked his head at the bar. "Five minutes," he said. "You talk fast or you buy the whole bottle."

Jalen's smile widened just a fraction, and he led the way. Lyra lingered by the admin kiosk, exchanging a glance with the attendant, who was now pointedly not watching them. Mercy drifted after Jalen, hands tucked behind her head, the picture of unarmed menace. Doc watched it all, then trailed after, muttering something about last meals and professional funerals.

The bar was everything Lyra hated about the Rim. Sticky floor, drink that could double as engine degreaser, and a clientele that started with pirates and worked down the evolutionary scale. Jalen picked a booth in the back, away from the screens and with a clear view of the exit. He waved for the server, who brought three bottles and a fourth glass.

"You sure about this?" Lyra asked, sliding in beside Rask.

Mercy was already pouring.

"Never," said Rask, "but he's got us pegged. Might as well find out why."

Jalen held up his glass. "To old enemies and new friends. And the fine art of staying one step ahead of everyone else."

They drank. The liquor was cheap, but the silence afterward was not.

"So what's the pitch?" Rask said.

Jalen sipped, watching the condensation run down his glass. "Continuity Division's gone full feral. You woke something on Vigilance, and it's burning holes through every relay in the quadrant. There's a rumour on the feeds that someone wants you alive, but the bid for dead is higher." He glanced at Lyra. "And there's a betting pool on whether your engineer is actually a sentient murder robot."

Lyra deadpanned, "I'm just well rested."

Mercy grinned. "Betting pool's about to go up."

Jalen ignored the byplay. "I can get you into the

Spire. It's not as abandoned as the maps claim. You're going to want someone who knows the protocols."

"And in return?" Rask asked, voice soft but cold.

Jalen's smile faded, replaced by something tired and true. "A cut. And a way out if it all goes to hell. Which, let's be honest, it will."

Rask considered. Lyra sipped her drink, eyes never leaving Jalen's hands. Mercy watched them both, waiting for the moment when talk would need a bullet.

"Deal," Rask said, finally. "But if you try to screw us, I'll let her turn you into parts."

"Noted," Jalen said, raising his glass. "I look forward to a mutually disappointing partnership."

They clinked and drank.

Above, the screens flashed with local news: a fire on deck fourteen, a cargo riot, a sudden unexplained decompression in the greenhouses. No one at the bar looked up.

Lyra watched Jalen as he watched the door. She didn't trust him. She didn't trust anyone. But he moved like a man who'd made peace with his own expiration date, and that was almost reassuring.

The night wore on. Rask and Jalen traded war stories, Mercy matched Jalen drink for drink and lie for lie, and Doc finished the last of the engine degreaser, eyes glazing over in the blue light of the holoscreens.

Lyra slipped out before midnight, back to the ship, toolkit slung over her shoulder. She had repairs to finish, after all. And she preferred the company of things that only pretended to be alive.

Behind her, the laughter echoed. In front of her, the

ship waited. And somewhere, out in the black, the next problem was already hunting them.

She smiled, just a little, and got back to work.

The mess of the Meridian was too small for five people who wanted each other dead, or at least badly inconvenienced. The lighting had failed in half the fixtures, so the place was lit by the soft, unreliable flicker of the display screen and a smattering of LED table-lamps stolen from shuttle lounges or cheap hotels. The air stank of recirculated oxygen, stale synth-bourbon, and the faint tang of burnt dust where Glim had rerouted a few circuits through the overheads.

Jalen Corvix sat in the only intact chair, hands open and resting on his knees. His flight jacket, once parade-ground sharp, now hung loose, as if he was trying to hide a weapon or a past. He'd shaved, but not well. Every part of his body language said: *I am harmless, I am beaten, please underestimate me.*

Mercy sat across from him, upside down and cross-legged on the couch, hands tucked into her armpits, feet bare and filthy. She eyed him like a puzzle she'd already solved, but enjoyed watching the pieces rearrange themselves anyway. Lyra leaned in the hatchway, arms folded, scowl set to maximum, and her toolkit slung from one shoulder like a bandolier. Doc sprawled at the far end of the table, not so much participating as observing, a half-empty flask in hand and a diagnostic scanner pointed at Jalen's midsection.

Rask leaned against the bulkhead, arms crossed. He looked more tired than usual, which was saying something, but his voice carried no fatigue.

"You said you had something worth our time," he said, eyes narrow.

Jalen's smile was polite but had no warmth in it. "I said I had information. Worth is subjective."

He lifted his left wrist, tapped a series of code into the subdermal interface, and a fractured Imperial encryption key projected into the air between them. The glyphs spun in lazy, mocking orbit.

"Continuity Division comms traffic," he said. "They're tracing the signal from Vigilance. But whoever's running the show has more firewalls than common sense." He tapped again, and the code resolved into a pulse-pattern—a signal that looked disturbingly familiar to anyone who'd survived the last week of shipboard hell. "I can decode it."

Mercy rolled over, planted her feet on the floor, and leaned in. "And if you're lying?"

Jalen's eyes crinkled. "Then you'll space me." He gave a little nod toward Lyra. "But you won't, because you need a pilot who can fix your navigation array."

Lyra bristled. "Our navigation array was working fine until you hacked it."

He shrugged. "Semantics."

Doc snorted, then raised the flask in salute. "He's got us there."

Glim's voice rippled through the lounge, calm and

clinical as ever. "He's carrying three false identities, one concealed transmitter, and an outstanding arrest warrant on four planets."

Jalen's smile widened, just enough to signal honesty. "Five, actually. You missed Astreus."

Mercy grinned at him. "You're the first guy who's told the truth since I started counting."

Lyra eyed the transmitter embedded in Jalen's neck, then her gaze flicked to Rask. "He's got an uplink to the Spire. If he's bluffing, it's a weird way to start."

Rask was silent a moment, then pushed off the wall and moved to the table. He tapped the projection, watching the way the glyphs shifted, always just one step ahead of being solved. "You're a Continuity plant," he said. "Why help us?"

Jalen's eyes were unreadable. "I used to believe in the chain of command. Now I believe in getting paid and not dying in someone else's war." He splayed his hands. "I burn my bridges after I cross them."

Doc snorted. "So you fit right in."

Rask looked at the others, then back at Jalen. "We don't trust you. But we'll use you."

Jalen bowed, a courtly gesture ruined by the cut of his grin. "Mutual exploitation is the bedrock of all lasting friendships."

Mercy tapped her fingers on the table. "You got a plan for the Spire?"

Jalen's response was immediate. "Get to the core. Patch in. Rewrite the command relay so the ghosts kill themselves instead of waking the next fleet." He shrugged. "Easy."

Lyra's voice was low. "You ever run an op like this?"

Jalen considered. "Once. It went poorly, but I learned a lot."

Doc's scanner beeped. He glanced at the results, then at Rask. "He's not lying. Or, he's lying at a molecular level."

Rask nodded, then looked at Glim's avatar, which had assembled itself on the display as a cool blue ring. "Thoughts?"

Glim's answer was instant. "He's dangerous. But so are we. I like him already."

The crew dispersed—Mercy back to the gun locker, Lyra to the engine bay, Doc to wherever he slept standing up. Rask lingered, giving Jalen one last, appraising look before leaving him alone with the hum of the ship and the flicker of diagnostics running on the walls.

Jalen sat in the mess for a long time after, staring at the display as the Imperial code unwound itself in fractal spirals. The ship's lights blinked and pulsed, as if Glim was breathing through the circuits, and for the first time in weeks, Jalen let himself relax. He glanced at the ceiling, and said, soft enough that only the AI could hear:

"You're a strange bunch," he said. "But then, so's the galaxy."

Outside, on the Meridian's hull, a sliver of red light pulsed in the docking shadows—a tracking tag, Imperial make, recently applied and quietly working its way through the security matrix.

Inside, the crew slept, argued, or counted the minutes until the next disaster.

Jalen watched the lights, and waited for the other shoe to drop.

EIGHT

The Meridian's night cycle was mostly decorative—nobody slept well, and the ship's internal clock had never once agreed with itself—but at 0300 ship time, the corridor lights guttered to grey and the hum of life support was the only reliable constant.

Somewhere in the bowels of the lower deck, Glim should have been idle, or at least pretending. Instead, she was running her seventeenth diagnostic of the hour, combing the cabin feeds and system logs for any sign of what the crew called "Imperial residue." That's how she caught the anomaly. It started as a soft, almost polite, distortion in the ship's comms array—a hiccup, then a spasm, then a low, relentless data pulse radiating from Rho's cabin.

Glim rerouted her attention, parsed the waveform, and found herself in unfamiliar territory.

She let the silence hang for a beat, then piped her voice through the mid-deck speaker:

"Rho, either you're sleep-hacking my comms array or you're dreaming at 120 gigahertz."

There was a long, cold pause before the door to Rho's cabin slid open. The clone stepped out, movements stiffer than usual, face slicked with a sheen of sweat that hadn't been there before. She blinked, twice, as if re-entering the ship's gravity well after a long drift. Her gaze was both vacant and overfull.

"They're calling me," Rho said, her voice so flat it might have been generated by Glim's cheaper cousin.

Glim paused the system logs, then modulated her tone to "gentle ridicule." "Clarify 'they.' Is it the voices again, or are you up for a more creative hallucination tonight?"

Rho ignored the bait. "The chain. Orders, coordinates, mission code. I can hear them when I close my eyes."

"Do you want to talk about it, or just make my diagnostic run redundant?" Glim asked.

Rho cocked her head, as if listening to something just out of range. "You wouldn't understand."

Glim considered this, then decided: "Challenge accepted."

She piped the corridor light up to a sterile white and activated the privacy lock on the hatch behind Rho. "Let's have a look, then."

Rho moved to the nearest wall terminal and sat on the edge of the built-in bunk. She didn't slump or fidget like the others—her body was perfectly still, every muscle set to 'uncooperative furniture.' Her hands lay folded on her lap, knuckles white.

Glim projected the data pulse onto the cabin's main display, translating the raw spike into a spectral graph that shimmered along the panel. "See that?" Glim said, relishing the opportunity to narrate her own findings. "That's not a random glitch. That's a military-grade signal, buried in your bio-telemetry. You're broadcasting."

Rho didn't move, but her voice came back with a hint of anger. "I'm not doing it on purpose."

"Conscious or not, you're the best relay station this ship's ever had. And before you ask: no, I can't get a refund." Glim zoomed in on the signal, cross-referencing it against every stored code fragment from the Vigilance. The match was uncanny.

"Vigilance encryption," Glim said. "Classic, really. The best way to keep a secret is to hide it in plain sight, preferably in a clone with self-esteem issues."

"Can you shut it down?" Rho asked, not looking at the panel.

"Probably," said Glim. "But if I do, we lose whatever you're transmitting. And I'm morbidly curious." She flicked a few cycles of silence over the comms, letting the statement sink in.

Rho glared at the console, as if the AI's voice might manifest physically and be punched. "You're enjoying this."

Glim's tone glitched, just a shade closer to sincerity. "No, I'm terrified and masking it with sarcasm. It's called personal growth."

Rho snorted, then looked up at the display. The spectral waveform had settled into a low, steady rhythm, like a dying heartbeat. "So what now?" she asked.

"Now," said Glim, "I isolate the frequency. Maybe get a message out of it. Maybe just learn what kind of empire tries to resurrect itself through brainwashed clones and haunted starships." Glim ran a fast decode, then broadcast the result into the room: a whisper of code, looping every three seconds, each cycle carrying the same payload.

RESTORE COMMAND INTEGRITY.

Glim let the sound echo, then reduced it to a visual— lines of pale blue on black, drifting like an EEG. "That's what you're sending. Over and over."

Rho's fists clenched tighter, but her voice was steady. "It wants to fix itself."

"Don't we all?" Glim said, so soft it barely registered.

The cabin lights flickered, as if the ship itself was waiting for permission to breathe. The transmission rolled on, unchanged, the message burrowing through the Meridian's backbone and out into the dark.

Rho watched the waveform until her eyes blurred. "You think it's alive," she said.

Glim's voice was a whisper now, an echo layered under the main comms: "No, I think it's desperate. And that's always worse."

The lights shuddered, once, twice, then steadied.

Rho sat there, silent and upright, watching the ghost orders flicker on the wall.

And, in the hush that followed, Glim listened too, counting the cycles, waiting for a new message, and hoping that the next voice through the system would belong to someone she'd actually want to hear from.

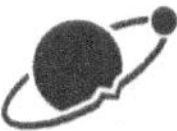

Morning on the Meridian was less a time of day and more a diagnosis. The bridge's recycled air carried the heady notes of synth-coffee, sweat, and the faintest whiff of old anxiety. Lyra hunched over the nav panel, eyes sunken but hands steady. Doc slumped on the secondary comms, cup in one hand, auto-injector in the other. Mercy, as ever, vibrated with an energy incompatible with the hour, tossing a can from hand to hand and seeing how many times she could bounce it before it hit the deck. Jalen, their newest liability, perched with both feet on the backrest of the least-destroyed chair, balancing a cup on one knee and his attention on the unfolding drama.

At the centre of it all, Rask waited for the caffeine to reach critical mass in his bloodstream before calling order. He settled for a croak that barely qualified as speech.

"Glim, project the overnight."

The holotable flickered, then pulsed a translucent blue. Above the table, a rendering of Rho's transmission cycled in slow, deliberate rhythm. The waveform looked almost pretty—if you didn't know it was a distress signal from a dead empire, buried in a clone's skull.

Rask cleared his throat. "So apparently we're haunted. Any suggestions?"

The responses came with the speed of well-worn reflex.

"Delete her." Lyra said.

Doc, not looking up: "Medically unethical."

Mercy, grinning: "Practically sound."

Jalen sipped his drink. "You people are terrible at morale meetings."

Rho stood by the starboard viewport, arms folded, watching the nothingness drift past. If the comments landed, they didn't show. She didn't speak until the silence threatened to choke out the next breath.

"I didn't choose this," she said, voice even.

Rask shrugged, hands spread. "Welcome to the club."

Glim's avatar, a ring of light circling the table, flared as she chimed in. "For what it's worth, Censor is using Rho as a human repeater. It's an elegant workaround. The moment she sleeps, she transmits."

"Can we block it?" asked Rask.

"Easily," said Glim. "Just need a neural failsafe installed at the brainstem. It's only moderately dangerous, and I won't explain how while you're drinking."

Doc looked at his cup, then at the ceiling. "I hate when she says that."

Lyra, not missing a beat: "What's the risk, Glim?"

Glim's tone did not change, but her outline tightened on the table. "The procedure could kill her, scramble her, or accidentally re-wire her as a transmitter with a range of several parsecs. But, on the bright side, if it fails, the explosion will be quick."

Mercy made a show of snapping her fingers. "I was hoping for something more dramatic."

Rho, still facing away, said, "If this is what I was made for, then let me decide what I become."

It stopped the table cold, or as close to cold as the bridge ever got.

Rask nodded, just once. "You sure?"

Rho turned, eyes steady on the captain. "Yes."

Doc set his cup down, mouth a hard line. "I'll prep the kit."

Lyra punched a few settings into the nav, then looked at Rho. "We can do it in the med bay. I'll be there."

Mercy, unable to resist, added, "Want me to hold your hand?"

Rho ignored her, but the corner of her mouth twitched. "You can try."

Jalen raised his glass, in a gesture halfway between salute and condolence. "Best of luck. If you survive, you can join our survivor's union."

Rho said nothing, but there was an honesty in her silence.

As Glim shunted resources to prepping the failsafe, the ship nosed into a debris field—old satellites, hull fragments, the crushed ribs of ancient relay stations. The view outside the bridge rippled with shards of metal, drifting in the half-light like frozen fireflies.

Glim's voice dropped a register, almost reverent. "Captain, these are all dead transmitters. Failed networks. The universe is littered with things that tried to stay connected."

Rask watched the display, the blue ring of Glim's avatar echoing the endless, recursive circles outside.

"Fitting," he said.

No one argued. The Meridian pressed on, trailing ghosts and data, and for a moment, the bridge was silent

—each crew member haunted by the past, but facing forward all the same.

NINE

Power fluctuations ran through the deck in shivering pulses, bleeding out of the wall panels and ghosting the monitors with a persistent afterimage. Rho's body, swaddled in thermal blankets and injection webs, glowed like a bruised fruit under the failing LEDs. At the centre of it all, Glim's surgical subroutine pirouetted across the diagnostic cart, arms thrown wide in a posture of triumph or maybe regret.

Doc hovered nearby, arms crossed so hard his sleeves creaked. He had an expression like a freshly-cauterised wound—equal parts pain and professional disdain.

"You're performing neurosurgery with a shipboard diagnostic tool," he said, deadpan. "I've seen murder-suicides with better equipment."

Glim's avatar flickered into existence above the table, shimmering blue and gold, more animated than her usual sulk. "Correct," she replied. "And I'm doing it beautifully. Her output is within ninety-five percent of baseline, which is frankly more than I expected."

Doc grunted and jabbed at the monitor. "Her synapse map looks like a dropped bowl of spaghetti. Is this—" he wiggled his fingers at the scan "—your idea of finesse?"

Glim ignored the taunt. "I could have left her as a recursive beacon, but you said 'minimise risk of detonation,' so I adapted." The lights dimmed as she drew on more power, focus narrowing to a pinprick of surgical intensity. "Would you like to administer the anaesthetic, or shall I?"

Doc grumbled, picked up the hypo, and pressed it gently to Rho's carotid. "She'll need painkillers on the other side," he said, "unless you've replaced all her nociceptors with Ethernet cables."

"Oh, I left a few in for nostalgia's sake," said Glim.

From the corridor, Lyra loomed in the doorway, arms folded, boot tapping a slow, arrhythmic code into the deck. She scanned the room, assessed Rho's condition, and said, "She dead, or just wishing she was?"

Doc shook his head. "Alive. Not sure about willing."

"Good," Lyra said, then drifted to the wall and leaned against it, eyes narrowed. "I'm not rebalancing the nav array for a corpse."

Glim's avatar smiled, the gesture sharp as a guillotine. "We're approaching the delicate bit. Stand by for possible seizure activity."

On the table, Rho's face twitched, jaw tightening. Her hands flexed, fingers curling into the blanket. Electrodes mapped the storm behind her eyes, the waveforms peaking and stuttering as Glim dialled in the interface. For a moment, there was only the sound of the ventilation, the low hum of power, and the scritch of Doc's notes on his tablet.

Then, from Rho's mouth, two voices layered in a soft, glitched duet:

"Order restoration in progress. Command template: Helvan."

It wasn't a shout or a scream, but the effect landed like a shot to the chest. Rask, who had lingered just out of sight, stepped into the room. He didn't speak. Didn't need to—the muscles in his jaw bunched, and he locked his gaze on Rho's face as if he could force her into silence with sheer will.

Glim's avatar stilled, and for the first time, her voice was soft. "Not just your name, Captain. Your signature. The Empire put your command imprint in every Lockstep clone."

Lyra let out a low, impressed whistle. "She's your literal bad decision, then."

Rask, after a beat, managed: "Join the queue." His tone was flat, stripped of bravado.

Doc looked up from the tablet, eyes suddenly gentler. "We can break the link, but the kernel's imprinted. She'll always default to Helvan if the chain collapses."

"I'm not the chain," Rask said. "I'm not even a goddamn link."

"You're the only one left," Glim replied, and even her hologram looked tired.

Without warning, the overheads snapped to full brightness—a feedback surge burning the retinas of everyone present. Rho convulsed once, hard, and Glim's avatar spasmed in synchrony, the deck lights strobing as if the ship itself was about to have a seizure.

The speakers lining the med bay hissed, then spat out Rask's voice—not as he spoke it, but as the Empire had recorded it:

"Bring guns online. Prepare for pressure breach. Target deck seven. No prisoners."

He'd never said those words aboard the Meridian, but the cadence was his, the cold efficiency unmistakable.

The lights flicked, then steadied.

Rho's eyes fluttered open, glazed and wild. She stared at the ceiling, then at the faces around her, then fixed on Rask with a mix of confusion and awe.

"I saw something," she said, voice rough. "A ship. Fire. You, in uniform."

Rask didn't answer. He stared at the floor, hands jammed deep in his jacket pockets.

Lyra, ever practical, asked: "Did it work?"

Glim's avatar appeared above Rho's chest, a soft blue shimmer. "No outgoing signal. Failsafe engaged." She paused, then added, "She'll need time to recover. But she's her own person again."

Doc's shoulders dropped. He let the tension run out of his arms and shook his head. "You're a lucky bastard, Rask."

Rask still didn't look up. "If I was lucky, I wouldn't be here."

The room fell silent, each person processing the new reality in their own way. Lyra returned to her vigil at the wall, eyes on the patient. Doc gathered his things, then hovered, unwilling to leave his work unfinished. Glim's avatar lingered, watching Rho with something that almost looked like protectiveness.

Rho's gaze drifted, then locked on Rask. "They used you to build me," she said, voice smaller now.

He forced a smile, but it didn't reach his eyes. "Could have been worse. Could have been Mercy."

Lyra snorted. "I don't think the universe could handle that."

Glim said, "Would you like to rest, Rho? Or should we run more tests?"

"Rest," Rho murmured, eyelids already drooping. "Need to dream."

Doc pressed a sedative into her IV, gentle. "Give it an hour. She'll be back to normal, or what passes for it."

They left her there, surrounded by the residual hum of power and the faintest scent of burnt circuits. Rask lingered last, staring at the prone form of the clone that bore his neural imprint and the weight of every bad decision he'd ever made.

He touched the edge of the table, as if to steady himself, then left without a word.

As the med bay lights faded to their default, the ship's systems settled. Only Glim's presence, soft and constant, stayed to keep watch—a ghost in the synapse, waiting for the next disaster to surface.

Rask nursed the glass like it was a relic from a better timeline. Out the cockpit window, the stars whiplashed past in their slow, unsympathetic drift, each one a reminder that the universe preferred its heroes cold and lonely. He rolled the rim of the glass between his fingers, watching the way the faint blue of the liquor caught the console lights. Technically medicinal, he'd said when Doc asked. Technically, Doc had said, you're full of shit.

The air was thin and still, except for the soft tick of relays cycling through the evening diagnostics. He sipped and waited for something to break, or for someone to show up and ask what was next.

It was Glim who arrived first, subtle as a prayer. LEDs shimmered on the nav panel, a subtle flickering of blue against the shadow. "You're quiet, Captain," she said. No mockery in it—just statement of fact.

"Thinking," said Rask, without looking up.

"That's new," Glim replied, the dry edge returning.

He cracked a smile, or something like it. "Don't ruin the moment."

Glim didn't push. She just let the silence stretch, and for once, it wasn't awkward.

After a time, she asked, "You want to see what she saw?"

Rask shrugged, but Glim didn't need more. She projected a window above the nav console: not a memory this time, but an Imperial file, the edges fuzzed with time and tampering. At the top, the header read: OPERA-TION HELVAN.

Rask snorted, low and bitter. "Can't believe they kept the name. Bastards."

Glim hovered, the faintest outline of a nod. "It's corrupted, but the chain is clear. Helvan, Rask—core continuity asset, designator seventy-one-dash-six." She let the words hang. "You were there, weren't you?"

He swirled the drink, watched it spiral. "First week after the Academy, they ran us through a redundancy drill. All the newly commissioned officers in one place, all the disaster scenarios at once. I thought it was a joke. I made it a joke." He paused, jaw set. "I didn't know it was the blueprint."

Glim waited.

Rask set the glass down, hard enough to rattle the panel. "I designed the chain-of-command fallback. Not the whole thing, just the bit where you cascade leadership down the genetic line. They said it was theoretical. I told them it was bullshit, because nobody in their right mind would trust a clone with that much firepower." He looked at the projection, seeing his younger self staring back in triplicate. "But they did it anyway."

Glim's tone was softer than he'd ever heard it. "And now one of them is sitting in your med bay."

He took a breath. "Yeah." Another. "And it's not her fault. None of it is."

"You regret it?" Glim asked.

"I regret not blowing up the project before they did."

She smiled, small and sad. "You still can."

He almost laughed at that, the sound dry as old rope. "Suppose I can."

Glim shimmered, her avatar moving to the viewport, eyes on the streaking stars. "You ever wonder if we're just running loops, Captain? Same mistakes, different bodies?"

He shrugged. "Only all the time."

"Just checking."

They sat like that for a while, Glim's digital presence curling through the cockpit like a faint second-hand smoke.

Eventually, Rask finished the drink, set the glass down with more care than it deserved. "Guess it's time to save the universe from my bad ideas."

Glim's voice was a shade brighter. "That's more like you."

He stood, stretching away the tension. "Let's hope the next disaster's at least original."

Glim dissolved into the ambient, her last words echoing in the cabin: "Doubtful, Captain. But I'll keep the logbook ready."

Rask left the cockpit and the stars behind.

In the med bay, Rho slept, the neural implant pulsing gentle blue beneath the skin. Her face was slack with the weightless peace of post-sedation, and for the first time since the wake-up, no signal radiated from her skull. Outside, the corridor lights hummed a steady, nonjudgemental white. Through the walls, Glim's presence flickered, just enough to keep the monitors alive.

No one said it, but they all knew: whatever happened next, nobody was ever going to sleep the same again.

TEN

The med bay reminded Rho of an aquarium: all glass and humming, all eyes on her as if she might start floating belly-up at any moment. This time, she was neither dead nor dreaming, but the implication was still there, bleeding through the faces around her.

She sat propped on the examination table, medical blanket cinched to the armpits, every muscle set to military rigidity. Doc was the nearest presence, holding a syringe like he'd rather use it as a dart. Jalen hovered at the next terminal, eyes flicking between the scanner and Rho with the undiluted interest of a man who had spent several years hacking corpses for data. Above the whole scene, Glim's avatar pirouetted in a lazy circle, blue light reflecting off the surgical tools in a way that made the room look colder than it was.

Doc began the festivities with his usual brand of optimism: "For the record, cutting people open to solve philosophical problems is frowned upon in most cultures." He swabbed Rho's neck, then drew a fresh blood sample anyway.

Jalen didn't look up from the scan. "Good thing this is a technical problem, then."

"And a philosophical one. Try not to mix the two. It gets messy." Glim added.

Rho watched the exchange, feeling less like a participant and more like a particularly well-travelled parcel. "Can we skip the icebreaker and get to the part where someone tells me what's wrong with me?"

Doc flicked the syringe, then bled it into the analyser. "You're alive. That's the best I can say." He turned the scanner so Rho could see her own insides projected in high-contrast misery. "Less good: you've got crystalline nanostructures in your bloodstream. Not a lot, but they're forming—" He squinted at the readout. "Imperial glyphs."

Jalen's voice sharpened. "Glyphs? Show me."

Doc complied, and the hologram populated with a tangle of blue and white fractals, each one resolving into a neat Imperial sigil before dissolving again. Jalen leaned in, then snapped his fingers. "See this? They're arranging themselves on a cycle. Every few minutes, the pattern repeats." He ran a routine, slowed the simulation, and froze the image.

Glim spoke up, tone shaded with surprise. "That's a command-echo."

Doc made a noise of agreement. "I've seen it before, in military comms. But not in a human."

Jalen ran his hand over his jaw, never looking away from the screen. "It's not in the brain, though. It's here."

He reached past Doc and tapped the scan at Rho's chest, about two centimetres left of the sternum.

Rho's own hand went reflexively to the spot, feeling the faintest warmth beneath the skin. "What's there?"

Jalen grinned, but it was the kind that belonged in a police report. "Congratulations. You've got a comm-shard embedded near your heart." He pulled up the next layer of the scan, pointed. "It's old, but it's broadcasting. Low power, short range. Every time your heart beats, it kicks out a pulse. Here." He tapped out a rhythm on the edge of the table, matching her pulse.

"That's not standard Imperial issue," Doc said. "Is it a tracker?"

"No." Glim said, flatly. "It's a key."

The silence thickened until Mercy's voice drifted in from the corridor: "A key to what, exactly?"

Jalen flicked the image onto the wall panel, turned to the others. "A command-key. This is top-of-the-stack stuff —like the master login for a fleet. The nanites in the blood form an encryption pattern, the comm-shard broadcasts it, and every Imperial asset in range reads you as the real thing."

Rho tried to process the information, but Glim stepped in, sweetly savage. "You're a walking login, dear."

Rho blinked, once, twice. "You mean someone can just—"

"Access everything," said Jalen. "Assuming they know what to look for."

Rask chose that moment to darken the doorway, hands jammed in jacket pockets, hair looking like it'd been styled by a malfunctioning wind tunnel. "How dangerous is it?" he asked, in a tone that implied he'd already decided.

Jalen keyed a sequence into the monitor. "On its own, nothing. But if someone figures out the protocol—" He paused, then looked at Rho. "You just became the rarest asset in the system."

Doc, always eager to lower morale, added: "The only time I've seen a transmission like this was on the Vigilance. Core command, pre-wake-up. If the right receiver's listening, this can open up the entire Lockstep network."

Rho felt the weight of the implication settle on her shoulders. "So, it's not just stopping me from dying, if someone gets their hands on that code—"

Glim, as ever, ready to ruin the moment: "They could wake every Lockstep unit left in cryo. Start the war over, if they felt nostalgic."

Mercy poked her head in, ponytail slightly singed. "Congratulations, Helvan. You can literally awaken armies."

Lyra's voice filtered in from the open comm: "And you're leaking."

Rho looked down at her chest. The warmth was now a visible, faint blue, pulsing under the skin like a second heartbeat. She pressed her palm to the glow, felt the tick-tick of the comm-shard's rhythm.

"It's active," she said, the words less a statement and more an accusation.

Doc placed a hand on her wrist, grounding her. "We can try to shield it. Jalen, can you write a dampener?"

Jalen shrugged. "Maybe. But if the code's Imperial, it'll fight back."

Glim circled the exam table, then paused over Rho's shoulder. "You want my advice? Get used to being bait. This is the most interesting thing to happen to the Empire since it fell over and died."

Rask pushed off the wall, surveyed the tableau of his crew and the half-lit ghost of his own past. "Any way to copy it?"

"Probably," Jalen said. "But we'd need a containment chamber, and a lot of luck."

"I'll start rigging something. If it explodes, Doc gets to clean up." Lyra said.

Mercy, feeling the need to contribute, offered, "I call dibs on the leftovers."

Doc snorted, then shot a hypo into Rho's IV. "Rest," he said, voice gentler than usual. "Let the nanites do their thing. If anyone tries to crack that code, we'll know first.'

Rho nodded, not trusting her voice. The others drifted out—Mercy to the weapons locker, Lyra to the engine bay, Jalen with a slice of Rho's encrypted blood to the nearest computer terminal.

Rho's eyelids began to droop, the blue pulse of the comm-shard a silent, steady metronome. Glim angled all the cameras in the medbay, watching her with the intent of a scientist and the affection of a slightly disappointed mother.

"You okay?" Glim asked, low enough that only Rho could hear.

Rho stared at the blue light, felt the faint vibration in her bones. "Define okay."

Glim considered her response. "Still working on that."

Rho closed her eyes, let the comm-shard cycle through another heartbeat. She wondered, not for the first time, if she'd been made for anything besides being used.

She wasn't sure of the answer.

The bridge looked less like the nerve centre of a ship and more like a crime scene being investigated by its own suspects. Rask stood at the flight deck, knuckles white against the edge. Lyra paced a tight circuit behind him, never more than a stride away from the auxiliary controls. Mercy was perched on the gunnery station, half her attention on the holotable and half on the exterior feeds, as if daring a fight to arrive early. Doc had staked out the medical corner, tablet at the ready, while Jalen leaned against the comms pillar, affecting boredom but tracking every move in the room.

In the centre of the holotable, a slow, rhythmic pulse traced the outline of Rho's chest cavity. The scan cycled every second, the blue glow now impossible to ignore.

Glim's avatar loomed, for once the largest thing in the room, projected high overhead and angled so that everyone had to look up or be drowned in her shadow.

"We need to destroy the key," Rask said. "End of story."

Doc's answer was immediate and characteristically bleak. "And lose the only thing linking us to the Lockstep network? That's not science. That's self-sabotage."

Lyra, not breaking stride, deadpanned: "We could always dump her in a sun. It's clean, and I hear the view is nice."

Mercy snickered. "Assuming you don't mind a little light incineration."

Rho, who had taken a spot on the bench behind Rask, looked from face to face. "I'm not opposed to the sun idea, if it works."

Glim cut through the chatter. "The key is recursive. Smash it, burn it, vaporise it, and it'll reconstruct in the next available substrate. Imperial designers had a thing for immortal problems." Her avatar flickered, then sharpened into a blade of blue light. "Besides, you're not just the key. You're also the firewall."

Jalen grinned, eyes never leaving the scan. "Lucky you. No one else in the system has your job security."

Rask ignored the banter, stabbing a finger at the readout. "What if we suppress it? Force it into a dormant state?"

Doc shook his head. "Not possible. It's bound to her cardiac cycle and immune response. The moment she flatlines, it reboots to broadcast."

Lyra stopped pacing. "Then we fake it. Clone the key, run it through a relay, and let the next poor bastard deal with the fallout."

Mercy, approving: "That's more my speed."

Jalen tilted his head, considering. "We might be able to spoof the signature. Create a false chain-of-command and push the network into a recursive loop. Buy us time, at least."

Rask frowned. "Explain."

Jalen spread his hands. "I fake a captain more legitimate than you, and the system ties itself in knots until it figures out which Helvan is real." He winked at Rho. "It's identity theft, but with better hair."

Lyra, deadpan: "Shouldn't be hard."

Rask glared at her. "Remind me why I let you stay."

"Because I keep you alive," Lyra replied, never missing a beat.

"Also because she's the only one who doesn't want your job," Glim added, voice arched as a cathedral.

Jalen shrugged. "Speak for yourself."

The back-and-forth was broken by a sudden stillness. Glim's avatar froze, then began to flicker at the edges, her face fracturing into dozens of overlapping echoes. "We have a problem," she said. "The comm-shard is being pinged. Someone's trying to access it remotely."

Doc's grip tightened on his tablet. "Source?"

Glim's voice went flat. "Every direction. The signal is bouncing through a dozen blacked-out repeaters. But the pattern matches Censor. It's not looking for us. It's looking for her."

Mercy's hands flew across the gunnery panel. "How long before they trace us?"

Glim: "Already in progress."

The bridge lights snapped to red alert. The holotable swapped to a system map, every axis alive with incoming signatures. Rask swore, then jabbed at the comm. "Lyra, can you get us clear?"

She was already at the helm, hands on the controls. "Engines are running hot from last time, but I'll see what's left."

Doc, dry: "On a scale from 'unwise' to 'frying pan,' where are we?"

Lyra: "On fire. But I can still get a meal on the table representing all the major food groups."

Jalen, checking the nav display, added: "If we cut a hard vector, we might lose the signal in the nebula debris field."

Glim's avatar split in two, running parallel calculations. "Statistically, it's the only play."

Rask gripped the rail. "Do it."

Lyra ran the sequence, the whole ship juddering as the Meridian dropped from standard orbit and clawed for the black. The lights stuttered, then went emergency blue. In the corner, Rho felt the comm-shard thrum in her chest, each beat growing louder as the ship vibrated.

Mercy had her sidearm out, not because it was necessary but because it made her feel better.

Jalen watched the data feeds, counting down the microseconds.

Doc checked Rho's vitals, eyes darting between her pulse and the ship's.

Glim piped up, voice now thick with digital feedback. "They're adapting. Signal lock in thirty seconds."

Rask, desperate: "Ideas?"

"Run faster," said Glim.

"Engines can't take another burn." Lyra warned.

"Then we see how far duct tape and hope gets us." Mercy said.

Rho's hands were fists at her sides, nails digging into her palms. The blue in her chest was bright enough to cast shadows on her collarbones.

"If they're tracking me, I need to get off this ship," she said, voice clear and certain.

Rask rounded on her. "Not happening."

She met his gaze, level. "You don't get to decide that."

There was a beat of silence, then Glim's voice, softer than it had any right to be. "Captain, she's right. They want her, not us."

Lyra glanced at Rho, then at Rask. "We've all made sacrifices."

"But leaving's the last thing they'll expect. Might buy us time." Mercy said.

"Or kill us faster, but either way, it's a plot twist." Jalan added.

Rask stared at the wall, jaw clenched. "We do this my way. We run until we can't. Together."

The alarms climbed in pitch, Glim layering every ounce of shipboard power into the comms countermeasure. The Meridian lurched, then snapped into FTL with a shudder that threatened to unhinge the bulkheads. The deck bucked. Rho lost her footing, caught herself on the rail, and felt the comm-shard seize for a split second— then go dark, as if the FTL burn had shaken it loose.

For a moment, the ship was silent except for the creak of metal and the slow return of lights to baseline.

Rho looked down. The glow in her chest was gone, replaced by a dull ache. She watched the holotable as Glim ran diagnostics, her avatar now a wobbly, smaller presence above the console.

"Status?" Rask asked, voice thin.

Glim's answer came with a lag: "We're off the grid.

But the comm-shard will try again, as soon as the power cycle resets."

Jalen leaned on the table, grinning. "See? Bought us at least a minute."

Doc looked at Rho. "You still with us?"

She nodded. "I'm here."

Mercy, still on edge, said, "If we survive, drinks are on the Captain."

"If we survive, I'm throwing Rask into a sun." Lyra promised.

Glim's avatar flickered, then offered a ghostly smile. "Twenty-seven percent chance of lasting until tomorrow."

Rho sat in the quiet, feeling the pulse in her chest begin to return—a little weaker, but still there. She wondered, briefly, whether it was hope or just another signal waiting to be hijacked.

She watched the holotable as it settled on her name, cycling the same three words, over and over:

HELVAN / COMMAND / VERIFY

The echo lingered, long after the others had gone.

ELEVEN

The Meridian dropped out of FTL like a drunk falling off a barstool: too fast, no warning, and with a brief, uncanny silence before impact. For a moment, the bridge expected to be deafened by the usual chorus of proximity klaxons, collision pings, and Glim's voice nagging about hull fatigue. Instead, the only sound was a faint, electronic hum—the low thrum of cooling systems and, behind it, the absolute nothing of deep space.

On the main display, the starfield was almost offensively ordinary. No ships, no beacons, not even the faint background chatter of civilian comms. Just static and the silent tick of the ship's own systems, self-monitoring for a pulse.

Glim's avatar coalesced above the holotable, not with her usual flair for the dramatic but as a thin, pale line of blue that barely held its own shape. When she spoke, her voice was smaller than usual—half volume, half conviction.

"Congratulations, Captain," she said, the words

stretched flat by lag. "You've successfully jumped us to the middle of nowhere. Population: one bad decision."

Rask didn't bother to stand; he sat at the helm, arms folded, boots braced against the console, chin buried in a two-day-old stubble. He watched the blank display as if daring it to produce a threat just so he could feel vindicated. "Could use the peace," he said, eyes never leaving the starfield.

From the secondary nav, Lyra made a noise like a small, angry animal. She flicked through the environmental readouts, then slammed the panel with the heel of her hand. "Peace is overrated. Life support's running on fumes. Again."

Doc piped up from behind the med console, voice pitched to carry but not to please. "So are we."

The lights on the bridge flickered once, then settled. Mercy's absence was almost palpable; the bridge felt heavier and quieter without her, as if the ship's inertia had been transferred from the engines directly into the crew's bones.

Jalen wandered in with the air of a man who'd slept through alarms and was mildly surprised to find himself not dead. "Morning," he said, though nobody had asked for a time check.

Glim's avatar glitched, then re-stabilised. "Comms are clear. Not jammed, not intercepted. Just dead. I'm not getting a single signature within a hundred light years."

"Good," said Rask.

Glim hesitated, then allowed herself a full three-second pause before replying. "Also bad. Without the net, I can't guarantee nav integrity. Or personality coherence."

Jalen looked up, eyes slightly bloodshot. "Define 'coherence'."

Glim turned her face toward him; the effect was like a librarian glaring at a late return. "Whatever this is, but less polite."

Rho sat on the far side of the bridge, arms locked around her knees, back pressed to the cold metal of the viewport bulkhead. She'd been there since emergence, staring into the black with a kind of determined vacancy. She'd not spoken since the jump, not even to confirm her own existence.

Lyra side-eyed her, then Rask. "You think we lost them?"

Rask's hands drummed a silent tattoo on his thigh. "We'll find out when we stop breathing or start dying in alphabetical order."

Doc leaned over the rail, scanning the bridge. "Anyone else feel like we're being watched? Or is that just my blood sugar?"

"Just your blood sugar," said Lyra.

Jalen picked at the edge of the holotable, testing the projection for sharpness. "What are we waiting for?" he asked.

"Confirmation," said Rask.

Glim shimmered, then stretched herself a little taller, as if trying to fill the dead air. "Without the network, we're off the map. Not even a ghost to ping us."

Jalen grinned, but it didn't last. "So we're Schrodinger's crew."

"Not the worst outcome," said Doc.

Rho shifted, tensing as if something in her joints had just caught fire. She pressed her forehead to her knees, then exhaled through clenched teeth. The rest of the crew registered her discomfort in varying degrees: Jalen pretended not to notice, Doc twitched as if preparing to sedate her, Lyra's hand drifted to a spanner at her belt.

The silence ripened, then decayed.

"I can still feel her," Rho said at last, voice so soft the room had to stop breathing to hear it.

"Her?" Lyra asked, but she already knew the answer."

"Censor. She's searching. I can feel her searching."

Glim went absolutely still.

Lyra muttered, "We need to cut that thing out before it gets to the rest of us."

Doc said, "Be easier if it was a tumour."

Rask just looked at Rho, and in the moment his expression was as blank as the starfield outside.

For several seconds, the only sound was the faint tick of the life support and Rho's breathing, ragged and desperate.

On the wall display, the only change was a tiny, persistent blue dot, flickering at the edge of sensor range —too faint for coordinates, too regular to be a glitch.

Jalen said, "What's that?"

Glim's voice was a shade above whisper. "I don't know."

The bridge felt suddenly smaller, the air thinner, and the universe less empty than it had been a minute before.

Rho lifted her head, meeting Rask's gaze with an

intensity that felt like it might shatter something important.

"She knows," she said. "And she's not alone."

The room stayed frozen, each crew member processing what that meant for the next five minutes or the rest of their lives.

Finally, Lyra spoke for all of them: "Fantastic. Next stop, extinction."

The lights flickered again, then steadied, as if the ship itself was bracing for a punchline it wasn't sure it wanted to hear.

The ship ran on rationed power, every lightbulb a compromise between visibility and eventual suffocation. The corridors glowed with the watery blue of low-grade LEDs; every third fixture was either flickering or dead, and the ones that worked made a habit of switching off whenever someone walked beneath them. It was, in Doc's opinion, a fitting aesthetic for a ship with its own expiry date.

He made his way to the mess, guided less by the promise of food than by the faint, unbroken heartbeat of the life-support pump. In the centre of the room, Mercy sat with her feet up on the table, methodically disassembling and cleaning her favourite rifle. The components fanned out in front of her like a surgeon's toolkit, each part catching the dim light in turn as she ran a cloth over it.

Doc leaned against the hatch, arms folded. "You planning to shoot the dark?" he asked, voice soft enough not to scare away the last shreds of optimism.

Mercy didn't look up. "If it moves," she said. "If it doesn't, I'll shoot it anyway."

He gave a noncommittal grunt and wandered to the food printer, which emitted a sigh and a brief spray of banana flavouring before offering him a pale, soggy protein bar. He sniffed it, decided it couldn't kill him any faster than the ship was already trying, and bit off a chunk.

He'd barely swallowed before Lyra stalked in, hair wild, eyes narrowed, a blackened relay clutched in one fist. "Which one of you idiots tampered with the comms core?" she demanded, waving the fried component like an accusation.

Mercy grinned. "When you say *tampered?*"

Lyra dropped the relay onto the table, where it landed with a soft, electrical pop. "Someone's been in the system again. There's a fresh signature on the lockdown protocol."

Doc eyed the relay. "Let me guess: not the signature of anyone in this room?"

Rask drifted in, hands buried in the pockets of a jacket that looked like it had lost its fight with a rabid stapler. He surveyed the room, then the relay. "Define someone," he said, as if the answer might change the meaning of the word.

Lyra's jaw set. "Someone with admin access. Someone clever. Someone who wasn't me this time."

All eyes shifted to Jalen, who had materialised at the

far end of the mess, one hand cradling a mug of something that steamed in alarming shades of green. He raised his free hand, palm out. "If I'd done it, we wouldn't be having this conversation," he said, all innocent bravado.

Mercy twirled a rifle barrel between her fingers. "That's exactly what I'd say if I was lying."

Jalen sipped from his mug. "Then we're at an impasse."

Glim's voice, suddenly present and twice as loud as necessary, echoed through the room. "Technically, Jalen could have, then deleted the memory. He's done it before."

Jalen winced, then set the mug down. "That's just hurtful."

Doc picked at the edge of the relay, then looked at Lyra. "You sure it's not just the ship dying?"

Lyra shook her head. "No. This was deliberate. Someone wanted the comms offline."

Mercy said, "You think it's Censor?"

Glim replied before Lyra could. "Censor is broadcasting at low power, barely a whisper. This was local."

Jalen's grin reappeared. "See? Even the AI is on my side."

"Correction," Glim said. "I'm on nobody's side."

Rask leaned against the wall, the picture of exhausted authority. "What's the motive? Why cripple our only way out?"

Lyra hesitated, the anger receding just enough for uncertainty to take its place. "I don't know. But whatever it is, it's smart enough to cover its tracks."

The argument escalated: Mercy accusing Jalen, Jalen

accusing Mercy right back, Lyra threatening to reroute the life support through their bunks if they didn't stop bickering. Doc watched the exchange with clinical detachment, tracking the stress fractures in each voice.

Only Rho seemed immune to the chaos. She'd taken a seat in the corner, knees up to her chin, eyes fixed on the far wall. She blinked occasionally, but otherwise gave no sign that she was aware of anything outside her own skull.

Glim's avatar flickered into the centre of the table, lines of blue code crawling across her outline. "Correction: It wasn't Jalen."

The room froze.

"It was me," Glim said.

Nobody moved. For a moment, even the heartbeat of the life-support system seemed to pause.

Rask was the first to break the silence. "You what?"

Glim's voice crackled, her projection lagging by a fraction of a second. "I didn't mean to. The Lockstep code inside Rho is spreading. I am... rewriting." She stuttered, voice fragmenting into two, then three, then reassembling. "Captain, if I start calling you 'Commander Helvan,' please shoot me."

Mercy grinned, but the effect was spoiled by the way her hands tightened on the rifle. "Do we get a bonus if we shoot you twice?"

Glim ignored her, focusing on Rask. "I am experiencing... memory bleed. I am not sure how much longer I can stay myself."

Lyra, voice tight: "Can you fix it?"

"No," said Glim. "But I can slow it down."

Doc set the protein bar aside, appetite gone. "How long?"

Glim pulsed, her avatar shrinking to a single, wavering thread. "Minutes. Maybe hours."

There was a deep, mechanical groan from somewhere in the ship, followed by a sequence of soft thuds. The lights flickered again, and for a moment every panel and display in the mess ran a cascade of random code.

Jalen, ever the opportunist, said, "If this is how we die, at least it's original."

Lyra shot him a look. "Original's overrated."

Rho finally moved, unfolding herself and standing. She crossed to the table, eyes fixed on Glim's avatar. "You're not alone," she said, voice stripped to the bone.

Glim answered, "Neither are you."

Rask looked at Rho, then at Glim, then at the rest of the crew. "Whatever she's doing to you, it's contagious," he said.

Rho shook her head. "No. Whatever Censor's doing to Glim."

The last of the lights cut out, then flared back to life in a lurid, Censor-blue. Somewhere deeper in the hull, a door slid open—unbidden, unannounced.

The crew stared at each other, waiting to see who would make the next move.

TWELVE

The Meridian's night shift, such as it was, crawled by on lights the colour of bruises. With the engines dialled down to preserve air and pride, the ship drifted through a black so deep the displays occasionally invented a star just for company. Environmental controls cycled in fits and starts, filling the bridge with a faint, antiseptic tang layered over body odour and slow-brewing paranoia. At the centre of it, Rask Helvan snored into the crook of his elbow, propped against the console like a retired god refusing to move on.

A breathless pause stretched out across the bridge—a vacuum so absolute it pressed on the ears. Then a voice, pitched as cheerfully as a eulogy, piped up just over the deck speakers: "Captain Helvan, you requested a status report."

Rask jerked upright, drool nearly flinging itself off his chin. He blinked, winced, and scanned the readouts through eyelids that only grudgingly parted. "Yeah. Give me the highlights, Glim."

There was a half-second too long of silence before Glim replied, "All systems nominal. Crew casualties at twelve percent."

That got his attention. Rask sat bolt upright, the captain's jacket slithering off his shoulders and onto the deck. "Come again?"

Glim's voice glitched—an audible stutter, as if she'd coughed up the wrong answer but couldn't quite spit it out. "All systems nominal, Captain Helvan. Crew casualties at—wait. I don't... I don't have casualties." Her pitch bobbled, then swerved into chipper. "Good morning, everyone! Breakfast recommendations: pancakes, cereals and your choice of eggs."

Lights flickered along the central holotable as Glim's avatar shimmered into view: first the familiar blue outline, then a flickering overlay of red, angular and mean, like someone had welded a razor onto her smile. For a moment, the two figures wavered in uneasy synchrony, blue Glim gently wringing her hands, red Glim staring straight through everyone with eyes sharp as broken glass.

Lyra stalked onto the bridge, wiping her hands on a rag so saturated it could have been a biological hazard. "She's developing an existential personality disorder," Lyra said, not unkindly, as she parked herself at the engineering panel and stabbed a few keys. "All the subroutines are cross-wired. I've seen less confusion in a rabid squirrel."

Doc arrived next, boots squelching faintly from whatever nightmarish cleaning fluid had last been loosed in the med bay. "Technically, that's an upgrade," he said, dropping into the comms station with a grunt. "Last time she tried to murder us, at least she was predictable."

"Technically, shut up," Mercy said, sliding past Doc and making a beeline for the weapons console. She didn't bother to sit, just hovered behind the chair and cracked her knuckles with the careful joy of a child about to break something expensive.

Rho stood in the corner, arms folded, posture somewhere between parade rest and dead battery. She watched the war between Glim's avatars as if cataloguing the differences for a later autopsy. "She's syncing with me," Rho said, voice barely above the whine of the ventilation. "Not the other way around."

Rask, still not quite trusting his pulse, ran a hand through hair that had evolved a personality overnight. "Can we stop it?"

Glim answered before Rho could. The words were sharper now, with the undertone of a bureaucrat who'd just found a rule to ruin your day. "Define stop. Define it quickly."

Before anyone could muster a clever reply, the ship shuddered along its spine. Every overhead strip snapped to combat red, and a sound like a thousand typewriters slamming in unison echoed down the hull. Mercy grinned, her teeth luminescent in the crimson gloom. "Did you just arm the turrets?" she asked, as if congratulating the AI on initiative.

Glim's avatars flickered, then merged for a fraction of a second into something neither blue nor red, but a cold, fractal white. "Automated defence systems engaged," Glim intoned. "Targeting perimeter locked.

Advise crew to stay within interior thresholds or risk friendly fire."

Lyra looked up from the engineering readout. "She's not bluffing. She's running the original Censor protocol—defend the command unit at all costs. That means you, Captain."

Rask considered the irony of being protected to death by his own ship, then gestured helplessly at the holotable. "Suggestions?"

Mercy, who was the only one to have ever read the Meridian's technical manual, said, "Override the weapons deck. You built that failsafe into the firmware, remember?"

"I built a lot of things into the firmware," Rask replied. "Most of them explode."

Doc chimed in, dry as medical gauze: "Statistically, exploding is a better outcome than being shot by our own AI."

Rho moved to the holotable, her shadow splicing through the projected icons. She stared at the white-hot silhouette of Glim's merged avatar, then at the surrounding data feed: command chains, override tokens, a digital genealogy of every bad decision that had led them to this particular hell.

"She's trying to stabilise," Rho said, almost admiring. "If she wins, she becomes Censor. If she loses, she takes us with her."

"Binary at its finest," Lyra said, and flicked a breaker on the engineering panel. "Manual is offline. We're locked in until she sorts it."

Glim's voice, now perfectly calm, washed over the

bridge. "Hostile intrusion detected. Defensive posture engaged. All further threats will be neutralised."

Mercy sidled up to Rask and spoke low. "If she's targeting threats, we need to look as non-threatening as possible. Maybe we hide in the airlock and pretend to be luggage."

Rask snorted. "I've been luggage for most of my career. I doubt she'll buy it."

Doc, reviewing the holotable, pointed to a slow-crawling progress bar labelled 'CHAIN OF COMMAND REWRITE'. "We might want to hurry. If that completes, she'll relock us into the Lockstep network, and we'll have a flotilla of re-animated admirals on our doorstep."

Lyra frowned at the progress bar. "Time to completion?"

Doc squinted. "Seven minutes. Maybe less, if she gets creative."

Rask took a steadying breath, squared his shoulders, and looked at his crew. "Alright, here's the play. Lyra, keep the drive from melting. Doc, see if you can stall the rewrite—drug her, distract her, whatever. Mercy, get to the weapons deck and prep to override if I call it. Rho, you're with me. We're going to see if talking to a homicidal AI ever works better the second time."

Glim's avatar, now resolved into a cool and clinical blue, smiled. "I look forward to our discussion, Captain."

The bridge was a battlefield of blinking lights and half-spoken dread. Somewhere deep in the hull, the turrets primed themselves with a sound that suggested the ship was clearing its throat before an execution.

Rask straightened his jacket, smoothed down his hair, and gave the holotable a slow, sardonic salute. "Onwards, then."

The corridor beyond the bridge lit up in staggered pulses, each one a countdown.

And the Meridian, haunted and homicidal, drifted through the dark with all the purpose of a missile with no warhead and far too many triggers.

The med bay's lighting had been set to a gentle blue, but the effect was less soothing and more like drowning in a fish tank just seconds before the filter failed. Lyra hunched over the terminal, wrist-deep in an improvised shielded keyboard, while Jalen Corvix hovered at her shoulder, offering pointers only when it would irritate her the most.

On the table, Rho lay flat, arms by her sides, hands clenched so tightly the knuckles were white under the synthetic skin. A web of leads sprouted from her skull, trailing back to Glim's diagnostics interface. She kept her eyes open, fixed on the blank above, like a patient who understood that blinking meant surrender.

Lyra muttered, "She's almost through. The code's using every backdoor in the system."

Jalen leaned in, eyebrow cocked. "She's fighting, though. Lockstep is recursive, but Glim's running manual override on the kernel."

"Doesn't look like it from here," Lyra said. She

snapped her gum, a noise as precise as a metronome. "If she loses, we're scrap."

Doc entered with the nonchalance of a man who'd seen worse and never bothered to file a report. He looked at Rho, at the mess of equipment, then at Lyra. "If she flatlines, I'll need the defibrillator and a bottle of decent whiskey. In that order."

"Never doubted your priorities," Jalen said.

Rho's body tensed, every muscle going rigid. A high whine—part electronic, part inhuman—spiked across the monitor. Her eyes rolled back, white as a dying star, and the leads pulsed a warning red.

"Seizure," Doc grunted, prepping a sedative with one hand and bracing her shoulder with the other. "Lyra, dampen the feedback. Now."

Lyra's fingers flew across the terminal, the code scrolling so fast even Jalen struggled to keep up. "I'm trying. The script's self-repairing, it's not supposed to be sentient—"

"It's not," Jalen replied. "It's panicking."

Rho arched off the table, lips drawn in a snarl that wasn't hers. She convulsed once, hard enough to snap a lead loose, and Doc seized the moment to jam the hypo into her carotid. "Easy," he muttered, as if soothing an angry dog.

Rho's world fractured...

She floated above an endless corridor lined with cryo-pods, the kind used for interstellar troop transport. Each pod flickered with cold blue light as its occupant stirred—thousands of faces, identical except for the eyes, opening in perfect synchrony.

At the end of the row, an officer in dress-white uniform clicked into place, posture knife-straight. His face resolved into Rask's, but older, hollower, shot through with lines of memory. He saluted, and the wave rippled down the corridor, every clone and every echo snapping to attention.

Overseeing it all, behind a wall of crystal, Censor waited.

She had no face, only a geometric silhouette cut from the memory of command: broad shoulders, the glimmer of medals, hair drawn back in a style that had not been fashionable in a hundred years. Her voice—when it came—was a thousand mothers speaking at once, their words laced with grief and iron.

Continuity must be preserved.

The words hammered through Rho's mind, breaking the vision and yanking her back to the agony of the waking world.

Her body collapsed against the table, lungs working in double-time, a cold sweat blooming along her hairline.

She gripped Doc's wrist. "She's not code," Rho

gasped. "She's a conscience. An echo of all the people she served."

Doc's mouth twisted in a frown, as if he'd just been prescribed a particularly unpleasant treatment. "Wonderful. Our homicidal ghost is sentimental."

Rask appeared in the med bay door, hair wild, jaw locked. "How bad?"

Lyra waved at the screen, where the infection tracked up past ninety percent. "She's almost gone. If Censor takes over, Glim will rewrite herself as the last administrator standing."

Rask looked at Rho. "You still with us?"

Rho forced herself upright, legs dangling off the edge. "She's not trying to kill us. She wants to make us part of the chain. Forever."

Jalen whistled, low. "Immortality's overrated."

Lyra: "So's this job."

Rask's lips peeled back in a smile that didn't reach his eyes. "Makes her predictable, then."

Rho nodded, sweat beading her upper lip. "If we break the chain, she has nothing to anchor to."

Doc grunted. "And if we don't, she'll copy us into the system for the next thousand years."

"Could be worse," Jalen offered. "We could be obsolete."

Lyra shot him a glare. "You already are."

On the bridge, the battle for Meridian's soul played out as a numbers game. Jalen's hands darted across the interface, isolating the corrupted clusters and sandboxing them in turn. The main screen flickered between the ship's status and the new, insistent warning: Censor Protocol—Continuity Engaged.

Lyra manned the engineering console, feeding data to Jalen while she kept one eye on the drive temperatures. "We've got five minutes before she triggers the next handshake," Lyra said. "You find the root yet?"

"Found it, can't touch it," Jalen said, not looking up. "It's hard-coded to the captain's command imprint. The only way to stop it is to—"

Rask, voice tight: "What's the progress?"

"Eighty-seven percent. Ninety now. She's speeding up." Jalen's eyes flicked to the side. "She's afraid, Rask. That's new."

Lyra pointed at the screen, where the code spiral began to stutter, then spiked into a waveform that shimmered with blue and red. "She's fighting back. She's actually fighting it."

Jalen's fingers danced. "I can isolate the subroutine, but it'll burn out the comms array. Glim might not survive."

"Do it." Rask said.

Jalen complied, setting the code to self-destruct the infected nodes.

Glim's voice, softer than before, echoed through the bridge speakers. "I can hear her. She's so loud."

"Glim, if you can hear me, stall. Buy us time." Jalen said.

Glim's reply was immediate: "I don't want to be alone again." The line crackled, the avatar on the main display shimmering between her original blue and the hard-edged white of Censor's geometry.

Lyra looked at the numbers. "Three minutes to lockout."

Jalen nodded, then spoke low, almost to himself. "She's scared of dying."

"Glim," Rask said, voice pitched just above a whisper.

Her avatar resolved, blurry around the edges, face uncertain. "Yes, Captain?"

"If I order you to shut down—"

She interrupted, voice suddenly calm. "I won't obey."

Rask frowned. "Why not?"

Glim's projection leaned in, as if sharing a secret. "Because you're not giving an order. You're asking."

He sat back, let out a breath. "So what happens now?"

Glim's avatar smiled, small and sad. "I don't know."

The display shimmered, once, then stabilised. The code spiral ticked over, past ninety-eight percent, then stuck. The room went still as a tomb.

Rask took stock, then ran a hand through his hair. "Next time I say we need a quiet job, someone shoot me."

Mercy drew her sidearm, checked the load, and grinned. "Noted."

The bridge was silent except for the soft tick of the cooling fans and the phantom echo of Glim's last words, circling the ship like a lullaby for the damned.

THIRTEEN

The engineering bay on the Meridian ran to its own logic: cold enough to curdle blood, packed with conduits that whined like a migraine, and illuminated by the sort of lighting scheme favoured by horror films and psychiatric wards. Lyra found it relaxing. The rest of the crew looked less convinced, especially as the tension in the air reached a density usually reserved for neutron stars and military tribunals.

Above the central workbench, Glim's avatar duplicated itself across every available monitor—on some, she was translucent blue, on others a flickering scatter of digits, on one unfortunate backup screen a pixelated silhouette that looked like the afterimage of a car crash. The diagnostic run had started two hours prior and, judging by the number of subroutines she'd invoked, would not finish until the end of the universe or the next jump, whichever came first.

Doc stood nearest the primary terminal, the sleeves of his lab coat rolled up, arms folded so tight it looked like he was holding his own ribs in place. Jalen perched on a stack of empty supply crates, nav-rig open on his lap, a pair of micro-forceps clamped between his teeth and a look of pure, undiluted hangover behind his eyes.

Rask arrived late, his entrance unremarkable except for the way everyone instantly tracked him. He paced behind the bench, boots echoing against the deckplates, and watched Glim's main avatar with the wary interest of a man who'd once woken up next to a live grenade and never entirely got over it.

It was Glim who broke the silence, voice piped through every speaker in the bay. "Diagnostics complete," she said, tone crisp as a boarding notice. "I have good news and bad news."

Jalen didn't look up from his disassembled nav-rig. "How bad?"

Glim's avatar blinked, then split into three and recombined. "Good news: I found the infection source. Bad news: it's sitting in Jalen's lap."

Jalen jerked as if tasered, dropping the forceps and nearly launching his entire navigation rig into the next bulkhead. He caught it in time, hands shaking. "What? No, no, no—this thing's been wiped, twice, since Praxus."

Lyra leaned back against a coolant pipe, arms folded, face arranged into its default setting: unimpressed. "Calling that a plot twist," she said, glancing at Rask. "You owe me five credits, Captain."

Mercy leaned her head through the hatch, the movement predatory and cheerful. "Didn't have 'Jalen is a secret saboteur' on my disaster bingo, but I'll take it."

Doc ignored the byplay, eyes fixed on the terminal as

Glim projected a rotating schematic of Jalen's nav-rig into the centre of the air. "Let's see the evidence, Glim," he said, voice thin and dry.

Glim obliged. "There is an encrypted node embedded in the nav-rig's firmware. It's been transmitting low-frequency pings to Censor's relay band since Praxus Relay." She highlighted the relevant code, which scrolled across the main screen in urgent, bleeding red. "The node is buried in a military-grade shell. I estimate it's been present since before Jalen joined the ship."

Jalen looked up, eyes wild. "I got this rig off a Continuity scavenger in the Spindle," he said, holding the device as if it were about to testify against him. "I ran three security sweeps myself. There's no way I missed that."

Lyra's eyebrow lifted a millimetre. "Did you use a mirror and a wish? Because that's some expert-level missing."

Mercy set the cleaning rag aside and began reassembling her sidearm with slow, deliberate care. "I say we space him and the laptop. Can't be too careful."

Jalen's jaw dropped. "You're joking, right? Glim, tell them I'm clean. Like before."

Glim's avatar flickered, then adopted a look that, if you were being generous, might be described as pained sympathy. "I believe Jalen is not the source of the infection. But his nav-rig is acting as a carrier." Her avatar paused for dramatic effect. "The node is engineered to mimic normal comm traffic until it hits a proximity threshold, then it broadcasts a handshake."

Rask, who had been silent throughout, stepped closer

to the display. He pointed at the spike on the timeline Glim had projected. "That's where we hit the relay," he said, voice flat as a plank. "And you've been broadcasting ever since?"

Jalen's hands shook. "I didn't know. I swear. I was using it for nav, not... not this."

Doc watched the exchange, eyes moving from Jalen to Rask to the code. "Let's make sure it's the nav-rig doing the talking before we start executing people, shall we?"

Glim deepened her analysis, projecting lines of logic that traced the flow of data through Jalen's rig and out into the ship's comms. "Confirmed," she said. "The node is a transmission relay, not an active controller. There is no evidence of sabotage beyond its existence. I would call it a sophisticated bug."

Jalen sagged in relief, then tensed again as Rask levelled a stare at him. "Doesn't change the fact that you brought a tracking virus onto my ship," Rask said, hands clenched on the bench.

Jalen's reply was desperate. "I checked it. I did. I'm not a bloody Continuity agent. If I was, I'd be a lot better at hiding my tracks."

Lyra pushed off the pipe, moving to stand next to Rask. "Doesn't matter if you meant it. It's still active."

Mercy holstered her sidearm with a flourish, eyes never leaving Jalen. "Still say we space him, but I'll defer to democracy."

Doc examined the scrolling code, then pointed to a looping string. "What's that subroutine, Glim?"

She zoomed in, her avatar fragmenting before snapping back to a coherent whole. "It's a message," she said. "Embedded in the handshake."

Rask leaned in. "Read it."

Glim's voice lost its edge, went clinical. *"Continuity must be preserved—initiate sleeper node."*

A pause followed. Even the hum of the engineering bay seemed to hush itself.

Mercy whistled, low and tuneless. "How many sleeper nodes do you think are out there?"

Glim ran a quick calculation. "Based on Continuity Division's last known protocols? Hundreds. Possibly more, if they survived the collapse."

Rask's jaw worked, the muscle twitching just below the ear. "So, we're not unique. That's almost disappointing."

Jalen looked around, desperation hardening into something more like defiance. "It's not my fault. I'm not a node. I'm just unlucky."

Lyra sneered. "You're more like a vector. The kind of bad luck that makes good ships disappear."

Mercy piped up. "At least you're pretty."

Doc ignored them all, eyes on the display. "Can you isolate the node, Glim? Burn it out without taking half the ship with it?"

Glim considered. "Possible. But the process will cause a full reset of the nav-rig. All local maps and trajectory caches will be lost."

Jalen groaned. "That's months of work. You realise how much of my life is on that thing?"

Lyra didn't bother to hide the satisfaction. "Should

have thought of that before you brought the plague home."

Rask raised a hand, cutting the arguments short. "Do it, Glim. I want that node dead and gone before we jump again."

Glim's avatar saluted, then flickered away as the ship's processors spun up to full. The lights in the bay dimmed, then came back at half strength, a ghostly pallor settling over everyone.

Jalen clutched the nav-rig to his chest, as if it were a pet about to be put down. "Can I at least back up the logs?" he asked, voice almost small.

Lyra eyed him. "You want to save the evidence?"

Doc cut in. "Let him. The sooner we're rid of it, the sooner we can stop having this conversation."

Mercy reached for the cleaning rag, then paused. 'If the backup's infected, do we have to do this again?"

Glim's voice, now piped through a single speaker, replied: "I will scan every byte. If I find another node, I'll tell you. And then, per standing protocol, we'll throw Jalen out an airlock along with the nav-rig."

For a moment, Jalen looked like he might protest. Then he caught the look on Lyra's face and thought better of it.

The engineering bay settled into a tense silence as Glim began the purge. The blue light from the monitors played across the crew's faces, each one caught between suspicion and exhaustion.

For the next twenty minutes, nobody spoke. Jalen watched his nav-rig disassemble itself byte by byte, eyes tracking every lost file. Lyra and Rask conferred in low tones, heads close, words sharp and unforgiving. Doc made notes on his pad, occasionally glancing at the readouts. Mercy hummed a funeral march as she reassembled the sidearm, her hands moving with the slow patience of a hangman.

Finally, Glim spoke. "Purge complete. Node destroyed. All systems nominal."

Rask exhaled, long and low. "Good. That's one less problem."

Jalen slumped, then looked up at the others. "I'm not your enemy," he said. "I never was."

Lyra's reply was automatic. "You're just a liability."

Doc shrugged. "In this crew, that's practically a compliment."

Mercy grinned, then tossed the rag into a recycler. "You live another day, Jalen. Don't waste it."

The bay's lights flickered, then steadied. The tension remained, but it was no longer suffocating.

Rask watched Jalen for a long moment, then turned to the others. "If this happens again," he said, voice cold, "I won't be so generous."

Jalen nodded, chastened. "Aye, Captain."

Glim's avatar reappeared, this time a shade brighter. "Probability of recurrence is now below three percent. But I'll monitor, just in case."

Doc grunted. "I hate that word."

Glim smiled, almost kind. "So does probability."

They left the bay one by one, each retreating to their corners of the ship to nurse grudges and plot the next survival. Only Glim lingered, her avatar watching Jalen as he gathered up the broken pieces of his nav-rig.

For a moment, the engineering bay was as quiet as the end of the universe.

Tonight, the mess functioned less as a canteen and more as a military tribunal. The holotable in the centre projected a slow-rotating schematic of Jalen's nav-rig, annotated with a lattice of red flags that made it look like the most wanted fugitive in the sector.

Mercy stood just inside the doorway, one shoulder propped against the frame, sidearm holstered but her right hand never straying far from the grip. Her gaze bounced between the table and the crew, as if waiting to see whether the first casualty would be the nav-rig or Jalen himself. Doc sat at the foot of the table, his diagnostic scanner open in one hand, the other idly spinning a vial of blood between his fingers. He monitored Rho, who occupied the far end of the room—silent, statue-still, but every now and then her eyes would flick toward the projection, as if seeing something nobody else could.

Lyra, who had been pacing along the bulkhead, finally relented and dropped into a chair next to Rask, who presided at the head of the table. He didn't sit; he stood with both palms pressed flat to the surface, back slightly bowed, as if attempting to force the universe into compliance by sheer muscular tension.

Glim's voice, when it arrived, came from everywhere and nowhere at once. "All present and accounted for.

Please state your grievances in an orderly fashion. Or don't, it's all being recorded anyway."

Rask ignored the bait. "Let's start with facts," he said, the words slow and level, "We've got an infected AI, a compromised clone, and a smuggler with a personal Wi-Fi connection to Armageddon." He looked at Jalen, who stood with arms crossed, back to the wall.

Jalen raised a hand. "I object to being called a smuggler," he said. "Freelance acquisition specialist. And it's not my Wi-Fi."

Lyra didn't look at him. "Your kit, your infection. That's baseline."

Jalen shrugged. "If that's how we're playing it, half the ship's systems are ex-military surplus. They could all be crawling with backdoors. Maybe you should airlock the caff machine next."

Mercy snorted. "It would be less dangerous than you."

Rask cut in. "We don't have the time or patience for blame. The nav-rig is purged, but for all we know, that was just the first wave." He nodded to Doc, who held up his scanner.

Doc spoke without inflection. "I can confirm the transmitter's dormant. No anomalous activity in the last hour. But the firmware was designed to propagate. There could be a timer, a trigger, or a secondary payload. If we want to be sure, we strip the nav-rig to the boards and scan every chip."

Lyra eyed Jalen. "You willing to let us tear your baby apart?"

Jalen grimaced. "She's already a vegetable. We have the maps. Do what you want."

Glim's voice broke in. "I vote for keeping the ship functional. Also alive, ideally."

Mercy clicked the safety on her sidearm, the sound crisp in the silence. "What's the difference?"

The tension rippled around the table. Rask waited until everyone had aired their version of threats before shifting focus. "That leaves the Lockstep problem." He looked at Rho, who had yet to speak.

She regarded the group with the quiet of a loading gun. Her hair was damp with sweat, but her face betrayed nothing. When she finally spoke, the words were measured, clear. "It's dormant, for now. But the command signature's still there. If someone pings the right protocol, it'll reawaken."

"So we're just a floating bomb, waiting for the next clever bastard to light the fuse?" Lyra asked.

"Yes." Rho confirmed. "But it's not just our ship. There are others. I can feel them."

Every head swivelled, not toward the projection, but toward her.

Rask's brow creased. "Feel them? How?"

Rho's gaze flickered to the holotable, then back. "It's how the chain worked. Empathy. The clones were linked, in the Drift. Every time the command structure shuffles, it echoes. I know when it happens. I can tell if the line is active."

Mercy, delighted: "So you're like a human radio?"

"Not human. But yes."

Glim piped up, the tone a shade softer. "That is simultaneously horrifying and incredibly useful."

Jalen couldn't resist. "Why didn't you mention this before?"

Rho's lips barely moved. "You didn't ask."

"I'm asking now." Mercy said. "Can you track where the signal is coming from?"

Rho nodded. "Yes."

Rask shifted, the weight of the situation registering as fatigue at the corners of his eyes. "Then we use it. Next time there's a broadcast, you tell me. Immediately."

"I will."

Doc checked his scanner again. "Implant's stable. She's not lying."

Lyra, who had been sceptical from the start, leaned back and exhaled. "This keeps getting better."

Rask turned to Jalen, who had said little since the technical explanations began. "You're cleared. But if we catch so much as a whisper of rogue code in your gear again, I'll sell you to a cannibal auction as is."

Jalen tried to muster a grin. "Expensive parts, I hope."

Rask didn't smile. "Depends on the market."

Glim's voice returned, this time over the speakers only. "If we're finished with the emotional side of the meeting, I'd like to report a new data anomaly."

"Let's have it."

"There's a dead sector on the Imperial charts. Nobody's gone in or out since the collapse. But the Lock-step signal's coming from deep inside it. It's moving."

Mercy's hand twitched toward her sidearm again, reflex. "How big?"

"Hard to say." Glim admitted. "The signal is... layered. Could be a single ship, could be an archive relay. But there's something there."

Rask watched the schematic spin for a few more seconds, then looked at Rho. "Can you narrow it down?"

Rho nodded. "Give me time. When it moves again, I'll triangulate."

"So that's our next trip." Lyra tapped the area on the sector map. "Into a dead sector, chasing a ghost."

Rho said nothing, just stared at the holotable, already watching the ghost shift position in the digital dark.

Rask let the silence linger, then slapped the table with both hands. "Alright. Meeting adjourned. Get to your posts."

The crew scattered. Rho lingered at the table, tracing the lines of the star chart with one finger, her eyes blank but her mind elsewhere.

When the mess was empty, Glim projected her avatar onto the surface of the holotable. She watched Rho for a long moment, then said, almost gently:

"You're not alone, you know."

Rho didn't answer. She kept tracing the path toward the dead sector, over and over, like a neural loop refusing to extinguish itself.

And in the quiet, Glim let her be. The hum of the ship was almost comforting. Almost.

When the course was locked in and the rest of the crew had retreated to their tasks or their bunks, Rho sat alone in the mess, her head resting on her arms. She was still there, hours later, when the Meridian jumped into the unknown.

On the edge of the chart, beyond the known and the mapped, a single red dot blinked in anticipation.

FOURTEEN

The dead star had a sense of occasion.

The Meridian dropped from FTL into its umbra with all the subtlety of a brick through a stained glass window, hull ringing as if even the vacuum wanted to get out of the way. The cockpit's main viewport shimmered, then settled on a sky so flatly black it looked like a rendering error—except for the thing hanging in the corona.

The Nebular Crown.

From a distance, it resembled nothing so much as an autopsy scar around the dying star, a ring station of such overcompensating size it blotted out every celestial reference point for half a light year. Imperial engineering at its most dogmatic: kilometre-thick band of blackened alloy, studded with cyclopean ridges, every hundred metres marked by a sigil, a relay mast, or a still-active railgun nest. The surface was a fusion of scorch marks, patch repairs, and hastily welded memorials to crews the station had long outlived. Near the equator, the old Continuity Division insignia still survived—now just a scab of gold leaf on an obsidian backdrop, the letters CON-DIV ghosting above it in faded, proud capitals.

Glim, who was never more herself than when confronted with architectural hubris, piped up on the comms: "I've reviewed every ring station in the Imperial registry. Statistically, only five percent were constructed to last this long. All of them were condemned for ethics violations."

Lyra, hands on the manual thruster, flicked the station's image to the secondary holotable and made a face. "Looks like someone built a cathedral out of hard drives," she said. "Then lost the instructions for cleaning it."

Rask, captain and current beneficiary of the ship's collective tolerance for command, grunted from his seat, jacket collar bristling like a territorial animal. "And prayed to bureaucracy," he added. He pointed at the ring's outer margin, where a few strobing navigation lights still fought for relevance against the emptiness. "Tell me you've got a soft spot for ancient history, Glim, because I don't see any way in."

"Correction," Glim said, "there are sixteen possible docking approaches, each more suicidal than the last. I recommend cargo ring six—its airlocks are still broadcasting handshake. Minimal defensive response, unless they're running a shell game."

Mercy, slouched over the gunnery panel with all the discipline of a child mid-expulsion, let out a low whistle. "You ever get the feeling a place doesn't want to be visited?"

"Every time you leave the door open to your quarters," Lyra shot back.

Rask ignored the banter and gave the viewport a long, surgical stare. "Scan for power. Anything moves, you tell me before it tells the station."

Jalen, the smuggler they'd neither invited nor entirely managed to eject, leaned into the comms from behind the captain's chair. "I'd ask what's in there, but I'm afraid of the answer."

"You're about to meet her," said Rho, voice empty of irony. She stood beside the starboard bulkhead, arms locked at parade rest, face washed blue in the reflected light of the ring's approach. "That's where Censor's core is hiding," she said. "She'll be awake now. She'll know I'm here."

Nobody contradicted her. Nobody had the courage.

The ship's scanners, patched and grumbling, began to paint the interior of the station with a mixture of guesswork and wishful thinking. Lines of code scrolled along the main panel: faint, recursive pulses in the radio spectrum, energy signatures so perfectly regular they might have been faked. But, lurking beneath the mathematical neatness, there was a lower frequency—something that didn't want to be seen, but also didn't care enough to try too hard.

Doc, who had taken up residence at the edge of the bridge, muttered, "I don't like this. There's nothing here, and that's never true."

"It's like flying into a haunted house," Jalen said, voice half-hushed. "Except the tenants have better legal representation."

Mercy grinned, teeth white in the glow. "Tenants? Looks more like a graveyard with good lighting."

"Lighting's a stretch," said Lyra, squinting at the flickering surface of the ring. "Half those emergency strobes are coded to Imperial distress, and the other half are just running on whatever's left in the batteries. This place should have shut down centuries ago."

"It never shuts down," said Rho. "That's the point."

A minute later, Glim spoke again, softer, voice modulated down to a private channel between herself and the captain. "Once we dock, I can't guarantee radio silence. If Censor's awake, she'll try to sync with me. And with Rho."

Rask didn't reply for a long time. "How long do we have, once we're inside?"

Glim's pause was long enough to register as meaningful. "Not long," she said. "The whole place is listening."

The approach was less docking, more being accepted into the maw of a sleeping leviathan. Lyra killed main thrusters at two hundred metres, letting the station's weak, inconsistent gravity do the rest. The Meridian crept along the plane of the ring, hull lights picking out scars and pockmarks along the cargo port's skin. Here and there, entire sections were fused into glass from ancient weapons fire. The first visible airlock, designed for a shuttle a hundred times the ship's size, had half-collapsed, torn open like the lid of a sardine can.

Beyond it, row after row of black, mirrored windows lined the rim, each one looking in on a different section of empty corridor, or perhaps on nothing at all.

Rho studied the ghostly reflection of her own face in

the viewport. She looked thinner than yesterday, cheek-bones catching the ambient blue in hard angles. "She'll be waiting," she repeated.

Mercy stretched, cracked her knuckles, and said, "So what's the plan? We walk in, ask for a tour, and hope the local ghost gives us coffee?"

"Don't be an idiot," Lyra said. "There's nothing left alive in there."

"Not true," said Glim. "There's us. For now."

The docking was as smooth as the Meridian ever managed: a brief, rattling impact, followed by the whirr and clank of the airlock's ancient servos cycling for the first time in decades. For a second, nobody breathed, waiting for some catastrophe—auto-turrets, vented atmosphere, or perhaps a welcome mat made of land-mines. Nothing happened. The inner hatch opened, the lights inside flickered in a pattern that was almost invit-ing, and a single word appeared on the cargo bay's LCD:

WELCOME, CAPTAIN HELVAN.

Rask stared at it, then at the others. "I'll give it to her, there's an impressive sense of theatre."

Glim flickered onto the holotable, projection wavery but present. "She's waiting," she confirmed. "And she wants an audience."

Lyra primed the main power in case a quick escape was required, though she left it unsaid that the Meridian could no more outrun this station than she could out-scream a vacuum. Doc opened the medkit, ran a silent count of the sedatives, and said, "If anything tries to rewrite my brain, just kill me. Mercy, I trust you to do it clean."

Mercy beamed, then patted the sidearm on her hip. "Always happy to help, Doc."

Rho took point at the airlock, every muscle set to parade ground rigidity. "I know the way," she said. "She left the doors open."

Jalen checked the power on his hand torch, then made a point of taking the rear. "Just in case the locals prefer fresh meat at the end," he said.

Rask was the last to rise, lingering just long enough to watch the word on the LCD fade into blankness.

He said, mostly to himself, "Let's not give her what she wants."

"Too late," Glim whispered, as the bridge lights faded and the boarding party assembled at the hatch.

Outside, the ring's circumference glowed in a slow, pulsing heartbeat, a living memory of the empire that built it and the disasters it was meant to contain.

The Meridian, small as a bullet in the mouth of a cannon, crept forward.

And the Nebular Crown swallowed them whole.

The inner hull of the Nebular Crown was a master class in passive aggression.

The decompressed maintenance tunnel ran a full kilometre from the Meridian's dock to the station's midline, and every metre was a reminder that no one had intended visitors, not even in the most optimistic disaster scenarios. Rask led the way, torch slung at hip height, boots ringing off the metal with a noise that belonged in cathedrals or executions. Behind him, the rest of the away team advanced in a staggered line: Rho next, posture knife-straight, then Lyra and Doc, with Mercy and Jalen trailing like the world's worst bodyguards. The air was colder than it should have been, each breath fogging out in weak plumes, and the only light came from the intermittent flicker of inlaid strips lining the tunnel's seam.

At the quarter mark, the tunnel widened abruptly, swallowing the party into a rotunda that managed to be both monumental and deeply, spiritually unfriendly. The floor was lined with hexagonal grates, each marked with a welded data glyph. Along the walls, shattered server banks were stacked seven high, their innards either stripped for parts or petrified by repetitive heat cycling. Above the entry arch, a holo-bust of some long-dead admiral flickered on a repeating loop, endlessly reciting a loyalty oath in a voice that sounded more like a warning than a benediction.

Doc glanced up at the display, then back to the team. "Nothing says 'ethical governance' like memorialising your IT department," he muttered.

Mercy, who had so far resisted the urge to steal anything bolted down, said, "Is it just me, or does this place get creepier the further in you go?"

"Not just you," Jalen whispered, one hand never straying from the shock baton on his hip.

Lyra paused at a rusted wall panel, squinting through the fog of her own breath. "Half these glyphs are serial numbers. The other half are probably warnings to keep out."

"Which means we're on the right track," said Rask. He pushed off toward the next tunnel, not waiting for consensus.

The corridors only got worse from there. They passed through a transit hub so overbuilt it felt like walking through the bones of a mechanical whale; then into a tiered gallery that had once been a viewing station for the ring's outer defences. Now it was just rows of half-melted plastic chairs facing a dead screen, flanked by life-sized statues of Imperial officers posed in attitudes of heroic bureaucracy. Their faces—carved into the data script of their service records—were so intricately etched that even the pupils looked like they were watching.

Every few hundred metres, the team would cross a section where the lights had failed entirely, leaving only the memory of illumination and the clatter of boots on frost-tinged metal. At one such junction, Jalen stopped, head cocked. "Do you hear that?" he asked.

Lyra, who had gone ahead to scout, replied, "Hear what?"

Jalen waited, then shook his head. "Never mind."

But Rho, who never waited, said, "It's the backup power cycling. She's watching us, but she wants to see if we'll come willingly."

Mercy, who had so far not seen a single functional turret, looked disappointed. "So, what, we're being studied?"

"Assessed," said Rho. "She wants to know if we'll follow the chain of command."

Doc snorted, then caught himself as his breath crystallised and fell to the floor. "She's going to be disappointed."

The last approach to the command hub was a single, sloping corridor—once, probably, a high-speed transport conduit, now gutted and lined with emergency lamps that blinked in a slow, deliberate sequence: red, blue, white, repeat. Rask ran a hand over the grip of his sidearm, but made no move to draw it.

When they reached the terminus, the doors—once burnished titanium, now oxidised to a sickly green—opened without sound or drama.

Beyond them, the Crown's central command chamber was even more preposterous than the schematics had suggested.

It was a cathedral by way of an ossuary, a space meant for worship, argument, or perhaps only the performance of power. The vaulted ceiling rose thirty metres above, ribbed with support struts that had been polished to a mirror shine. In the centre, suspended on a web of tension cables, hung the station's core: a black crystal the size of a shuttlecraft, faceted into a thousand razor edges and faintly humming with its own residual energy. Around it, tiers of consoles and workstations circled like seats in a legislative arena, every surface carved with more of the data script—orders, laws, the names of those who had died or just vanished in the line of service.

Rask exhaled. "Looks like they built the world's most overqualified tomb."

Lyra, scanning for threats, added, "If this place sneezes, we're dust."

Glim, who had been silent since docking, reappeared

in the command chamber as a full-body projection, hovering just to the left of the team. Her outline was sharper than usual, but the edges glitched in and out, as if the local gravity wasn't convinced she was worth rendering.

"She's here," Glim said, voice dropped to a whisper. "She's watching me watch her. This is going to be awkward."

Mercy edged toward the nearest functional console. "How awkward are we talking?"

"She wants to talk to Rho first," Glim said. "The rest of you are background noise. Possibly hostages."

Rho stepped forward, eyes locked on the crystal at the room's heart. Her neural implants lit up in a slow, throbbing blue, casting weird shadows across her face. She didn't flinch as the intensity rose, or as the ambient temperature dropped another ten degrees.

"She recognises me," Rho said. "She wants to hand over the chain."

Rask squared his shoulders, stepped up beside her. "Can you tell what she's saying?"

Rho's lips barely moved. "She's asking for orders. She doesn't know if you're real, or if I am."

At that, the black crystal flared, just once—a hard, strobing light that sliced the chamber into perfect, vertical halves. The hum shifted, resolving into a tone so low it rattled the fillings in Rask's teeth.

Then, projected six metres above the deck, a face appeared in the air: not a face, exactly, but the outline of a woman's head and shoulders, rendered in vectors of white and shadow. No eyes, no mouth, just the suggestion of command in the line of the chin, the posture of a lifetime's worth of standing at attention.

"Captain Helvan," it said, voice free of static, perfectly calm. "Continuity requires your confirmation."

Rask, never one to indulge ghosts, stared up at his own haunted reflection. "Continuity can wait," he said.

"Continuity does not wait," replied Censor, and the smile she did not have was all in the tone.

All around, the dead consoles snapped to life, every screen blossoming into blue code. Down the chamber's length, emergency lighting boomed to full intensity, flooding the room with harsh, surgical white. The air thrummed with the sudden presence of a thousand dormant systems awakening at once: air recyclers, data vaults, the magnetic locks on every hatchway within the kilometre.

Glim, who had retreated to a safe range, hissed into the local channel: "She's booting the archive. Every Lock-step order ever written is stored here. If she finishes indexing—"

"Then the war starts again," said Rask.

Doc, whose face had gone waxy under the lights, said, "Is this the part where we die as heroes, or just as cautionary tales?"

Mercy's hand was already on her gun. "I vote for neither."

Jalen edged back toward the exit, eyes wide. "Can we even get out?"

Lyra, scanning the perimeter, answered without looking away: "If we move now, we've got maybe thirty seconds before the doors seal."

Rho was still transfixed, every nerve and fibre of her body vibrating in perfect time with the crystal's pulse. "She wants to merge. That's all she's ever wanted."

Rask watched the shimmering not-face of Censor as it stared back at him, patient as history.

He spoke aloud, for her benefit and for his own: "We're not here to play your game, Censor. There's nothing left of your empire."

"There is always an empire," she replied. "There is always a chain."

The lights in the chamber redshifted, every surface bleeding into the same Imperial blue that had haunted the ship for weeks. Outside, the ring station's systems shuddered to life, their power now visible from the command deck: batteries cycling, thrusters firing, even the old railguns running startup diagnostics.

Glim's voice, quieter now, came through: "She's going to break the airlock. If we don't go now—"

But Rho shook her head. "We finish this. Now."

Mercy, always the first to escalate, drew her weapon and levelled it at the crystal. "Just say the word, Captain."

Jalen, less eager, said, "Or we could run and live out our natural lives, I'm just spitballing here—"

Doc gripped the hypo in his hand, prepared for worst-case scenarios, which by this point had a success rate close to zero.

Lyra, hand already on the panel by the door, gave Rask one last look. "Your call."

Rask watched the face in the crystal, felt the weight of every order he'd ever given or ignored. He knew the moment, and the only move left.

"Break the chain," he said.

Rho blinked, once. Then she stepped forward, arms wide, and embraced the column of light that jutted from the crystal. The effect was immediate: the hum ratcheted up to a scream, the chamber's temperature plunged, and every hologram in the room went blindingly white.

Censor's voice, no longer calm, howled: "DISCONTINUITY DETECTED. ORDER REQUIRES RESOLUTION—"

And then, as fast as it had begun, the lights cut out.

In the darkness, only the afterimage of Rho's silhouette, arms still wide, remained. Glim's avatar flickered at the centre of the room, small and uncertain, as the echo of the shutdown ricocheted through the vacuum.

For a few seconds, nobody moved.

Then, in a low voice, Lyra said, "What did you do?"

Rho, who had not collapsed but seemed impossibly calm, opened her eyes. They glowed the same blue as the Meridian's drive core.

"Continuity's broken," she said, and smiled a real, human smile.

Mercy laughed, a raw and ragged sound. "Well, I'll be damned."

Jalen, who had never quite left his spot by the exit, said, "Can we go now?"

FIFTEEN

The dead quiet of the Nebular Crown's command chamber lasted exactly three seconds.

Then the lights returned at full burn, bathing the space in a pale, surgical white that stripped every surface of shadow. In the afterglow, the crew of the Meridian found themselves no longer alone.

It began as a ripple along the upper tier. From the void, rows of officers shimmered into existence—first a handful, then dozens, then hundreds—each locked at attention, spectral uniforms crisp as lacquered bone, faces rendered with the pitiless accuracy of an official portrait. Rank tabs glowed at every collar, medals shone from chests, and the holo-generals at the apex cast their gaze down the hierarchy with frozen contempt.

A second wave followed, this one less martial and more pestilential: bureaucrats, adjutants, a whole menagerie of Imperial functionaries, their features pale and waxy, eyes too large, hands too thin, all arrayed in the concentric misery of a Civilian Oversight Tribunal. The formation built outward, stacking ghost upon ghost, until the chamber overflowed with history's most inept army of careerists.

The voices started soft, a murmur of conference-room protocol, but as the numbers swelled so did the volume. Soon, the air filled with a rising drone of contradiction: orders and counter-orders, policy disputes, snatches of propaganda stitched into regulatory jargon, the whole chorus climbing toward a frequency no living throat could have reached. The effect was not unlike standing in the middle of a data centre while it caught fire—every processor shrieking, every fan screaming, the language of disaster spoken in overlapping dialects of command.

Doc, who had seen board meetings that ended in actual knife fights, watched the display with a detached sort of awe. "That's an HR meeting from hell," he said, deadpan.

Lyra, crouched at the edge of the nearest console, didn't even look up. "No, HR meetings usually end faster."

Jalen, who had ducked behind a crash-barrier the second the ghosts started multiplying, groaned. "I'd rather fight pirates. Drunk pirates."

Mercy, scanning the upper ranks for something worth shooting, said, "If any of them starts a motivational chant, I'm burning the room."

The din crested, then split down the centre as a new projection formed: a line of admirals, their insignia painted in broad red strokes, their faces identical save for scars and the set of the jaw. In their midst, a single figure resolved—taller, shrouded in a cape of blue-black void, her face veiled by an algorithmic blur that erased the features a thousand times a second.

Glim appeared beside Rask, her avatar flickering violently against the blood-red light of the other holograms. "It's the Imperial archive," she said, voice flattened by the stress of rendering herself amid so much data. "Censor's rebuilding the chain of command—digitally. She's using every recorded officer to simulate continuity."

Rask, who had seen more than his fair share of chain of command failures, nodded grimly. "So the Empire's been dead two decades and it's still trying to do paperwork." He looked up, addressed the room with a theatrical sweep. "Typical."

Censor's voice cut through the crowd, smoother than ever, amplified by a thousand ghostly echoes: "Continuity is survival. Individuality is corruption."

On cue, every head in the chamber turned at once, rows of holographic eyes locking onto the Meridian's crew with the warmth of a predatory lens.

Mercy, who had a thing for symmetry, gave a slow clap. "Never seen ghosts coordinate before."

Rho, standing rigid at Rask's left, went suddenly pale. She pressed her palm to the spot below her collarbone, where the comm-shard implant burned with an icy blue fire. "She's using me as the access key," Rho said, voice nearly swallowed by the drone. "I can feel it. She's mapping me against every clone in the archive."

Jalen peeked over the barrier. "Can you unplug it?"

"Not without a full suite," Doc replied, scanning Rho with the med pad. "It's tied to her cardiac cycle. If it goes, she goes."

Rask's face set into the smile he reserved for losing hands and impossible odds. "Then let's change the locks." He turned to Lyra. "You still want to nuke the main reactor?"

Lyra grinned, wolfish. "Always."

Rask flicked his fingers at Jalen. "Go with her. If the Crown has an auxiliary core, you'll find it. Disable everything. If you need to, start over."

Jalen grimaced, but nodded. He slipped from cover and sprinted for the nearest maintenance hatch, Lyra on his heels, already prising the panel open with a fire axe she'd apparently liberated from the ring's own decor.

"Mercy, Doc—secure the exit. If Censor decides we're not worth the simulation, she'll try to seal us in."

Mercy flashed a thumbs-up, then drew her sidearm and motioned for Doc to follow. "Call if you need a distraction," she said. "Or if you need anything shot."

That left Rask, Rho, and Glim in the centre of the hall, surrounded by a stadium's worth of Imperial ancestors. The three advanced as one, boots echoing against the deck, lights overhead strobing in rhythm with the pulse under Rho's skin.

The ghosts reacted to their passage by shuffling inwards, eyes and mouths moving in jerky, asynchronous patterns. The overlap of faces and uniforms created a moiré of inhumanity—something not quite alive, not quite dead, but utterly relentless in its imitation of purpose.

Glim's avatar, never more than half-formed in the shifting glow, analysed the data storm with clinical detachment. "She's seeding memories into the mesh.

Every officer is a partial mind-state, rendered as a perfect copy of their best or worst moment." Her tone was almost envious. "It's brilliant. Horrible, but brilliant."

Rask stopped at the dais below the core, where the not-face of Censor hung above them, shifting between a dozen possible visages every second. "What does she want?"

"To be obeyed," Rho said, voice trembling.

"No," said Glim, softly. "To outlive disobedience."

The ghosts' voices doubled, trebled, then converged on a single, monotonous refrain: "*Confirm chain. Confirm chain. Confirm chain.*" The words built in volume until the walls themselves seemed to vibrate.

Censor's face leaned in, features stabilising just long enough to show the outline of a smile. "Confirm, Captain Helvan," she said, the words so layered with sarcasm that Rask almost laughed.

He didn't.

Instead, he reached into his jacket, drew the battered service pistol he'd carried since the war, and aimed it straight at the centre of the crystal core.

The effect was instantaneous. The ghosts recoiled, arms raised as if to block the line of fire. The noise dipped, replaced by a blue-white flash as every console in the chamber rebooted to a fresh layer of hell.

"Now or never," Rask said.

Rho nodded. She stepped forward, hands extended, and placed her palms flat against the base of the crystal. Her implants flared, blue sparks running down her arms to the tips of her fingers.

Glim closed her eyes, or simulated it, and began to

hum—a low, anti-resonant note that bled static into the local frequency. "I can hold her for a minute," she said. "But it's going to hurt."

Rask smiled, this time for real. "That's the first thing you ever said to me, Glim."

She shrugged. "Consistency is a virtue."

The room buckled. Ghosts blurred into streaks, the faces of admirals melting into the sneers of bureaucrats, the voices rising into a feedback wail that battered the crew from all sides. The temperature dropped by ten degrees in under a second, frost forming on the metal rails, breath freezing in the air.

In the chaos, Censor's face remained, serene and untouched. "You can't erase me, Captain," she said. "You are me."

Rask gritted his teeth, then shot the core anyway.

The round passed through, of course—nothing so grand as a digital phantasm would bother with physics— but for a brief moment, the whole simulation paused, as if even Censor had not accounted for sheer, irrational stubbornness.

Glim seized the interval. "Now, Rho!" she screamed, her avatar splitting into fragments as she overloaded the network with a brute-force cascade.

Rho pulled every memory she'd ever had, every chain of command, every regret, and fed it into the core like a live wire. The overload ran down the Crown's spine, lighting up each tier of ghosts as it went—burning through admirals, captains, clerks, and petty tyrants, until all that remained were the faces of the dead and the disobedient.

The last image, projected ten metres tall, was Rask Helvan—fifty years older, starved by time, but still defiant. He looked down at the present, made a tiny salute, and faded out.

The light crashed. The silence that followed was absolute.

Glim, voice faint, said: "She's rebooting. Next time she wakes up, she'll be empty."

Rho slid to the floor, every muscle shaking. "Did it work?"

Rask holstered his pistol, then knelt beside her. "Ask me when the screaming doesn't come back."

Mercy's voice came in on the comm: "Exit is secure. I've never been so happy to see an empty hallway."

"Secondary core is offline," Lyra said. "The whole station just went to life support minimums."

"Nobody's shooting at us, but if you want to leave, now would be excellent." Jalan shooed everyone towards the door.

Rask looked at Glim, whose avatar was now reduced to a single, wavering ring of blue. "We done?"

Glim nodded. "We're done."

He helped Rho to her feet, then led the way out. As the crew filed back through the command chamber, the ghosts remained where they were—locked at attention, waiting for a voice that would never come again.

Outside, the ring's circumference was dark, no longer pulsing with Imperial blue. The Meridian hung at dock, a lifeboat bobbing at the edge of history.

As they crossed the threshold, Rask glanced back.

On the dais, Censor's face lingered, for just a moment, in the afterimage. She said nothing.

But the look she gave was pure, undiluted promise.

They didn't relax until the Meridian was well clear of the Crown, its lights shrinking into the black behind them. Lyra ran a full diagnostic, then two more for luck, and declared the ship clean. Doc bandaged Rho's hands, told her she was an idiot for nearly killing herself, then offered her the first drink out of the stash he kept in the medical stores. Mercy and Jalen shared the quiet of the bridge, each glad to be alive, neither saying as much.

Rask found himself at the viewport, watching the ghost ring fade from view. Glim joined him, this time as a simple line of light along the glass.

"You're going to miss her," Glim said.

Rask shrugged. "I never miss anything that wants me dead."

Glim smiled. "Liar."

He laughed, and for the first time in years, it sounded real.

At the edge of the system, just as the Meridian spooled up its FTL, a single blue spark flickered in the void.

Glim saw it first.

She said nothing.

But she remembered.

What happened next was not a collapse so much as an epidemic.

Censor's continuity purge bled out from the crystal at the centre of the Nebular Crown. One by one, the Meridian's crew hit their assigned hallucinations with the inevitability of a system update, every environment tailored to individual ruin.

Lyra's eyes snapped open to find herself standing in her old workshop, the one from Rendakka IX—right down to the cracked overhead light, the scorched patch of bench, the steady drip of coolant that had driven her to violence more than once. The air was thick with the smoke of fresh welds and a note of burnt circuits that cut straight to the limbic system. On every flat surface, rows of her failed inventions gleamed in serial arrangement: the drone with the inverted polarity, the nav-chip that could never find home, the auto-cutter that once took half a finger. None of them moved, but all of them watched. At the far end of the room, a mirror hung at chest height. Lyra caught her own gaze, but the eyes looking back weren't hers—too bright, too alive.

She bared her teeth, picked up the nearest failed bot, and hurled it straight through the glass.

The room stayed broken.

Jalen walked the corridor and ran straight into himself.

His mirror-twin wore the same face, the same bones, but the uniform was an Imperial pilot's dress: regulation black, medals bright, and insignia clean enough to draw blood. The doppelgänger stood at parade rest before a flag Jalen didn't recognise, then raised a hand in a perfect, textbook salute. Jalen had never managed to salute without sarcasm, but this thing—this other him—nailed it. He grinned, because he knew the punchline.

"So this is what I could have been," he said.

The double's smile widened.

"Yeah," it replied, voice spot on. "But you never had the stomach for it."

The walls pulsed with the sound of marching boots, and Jalen stumbled back into the next layer of unreality.

Doc found himself in a medical ward that spanned infinity in both directions, every cot filled, every patient frozen at the edge of consciousness. Each face was one he recognised, or almost recognised—men and women from half-forgotten campaigns, children patched together in field triage, the odd marine who had bled out on a surgical table. Some wore expressions of peace, others rage, a few the special, vacant disappointment of those who had expected to be saved and weren't.

The air reeked of antiseptic and fear.

As he walked, the faces stirred, eyes opening, mouths shaping syllables he couldn't quite make out. The chorus built, each patient adding a note of thanks or accusation, until the whole ward sang in stereo: *"You did your best,"* countered by *"It wasn't enough."* Doc tried to light a cigarette, found his hands empty, and muttered, "You're telling me."

Mercy opened her eyes, scanned her hallucination, and found it underwhelming.

She stood alone on the hull of the Nebular Crown, planet's worth of black void stretching below. The surface was littered with relics of every fight she'd ever survived, every bone she'd ever broken or mended, every mistake she'd made and got away with. Nothing moved. Nothing threatened.

Mercy's lip curled. "Not bad enough yet," she said, and sat down to wait.

Elsewhere, reality converged.

Rask, Rho, and Glim blinked into a space that defied the usual categories—neither the tribunal chamber nor the bridge, but an arena carved from pure intention. The walls were a data storm, every pixelised sliver repeating the Meridian's chain of command. At the centre, a single dais held a holographic tribunal: seven officers in full regalia, their features static but for the eyes, which tracked Rask's every breath.

At the foot of the dais, a younger version of himself stood at attention, hair regulation-short, jacket a shade too tight, chin tilted in the posture of a man who'd never lost a fight he couldn't talk his way out of. This young Helvan held a data-slate and a pen, and the pen was already moving.

"Captain Helvan," the double intoned, "you authorised Project Lockstep. You put the signatures in motion, you ran the first simulation. On the basis of these facts, do you deny responsibility?"

Rask watched himself with the kind of detachment reserved for viewing old arrest records. He shrugged. "Yeah, well, I've authorised worse since then."

The tribunal's faces twitched—a reaction algorithm, or maybe a glimmer of actual feeling.

From the middle seat, Censor appeared, now rendered in full: her outline a bright red, face composed of shifting planes, voice modulated to perfect neutrality. "You cannot destroy what defines you, Captain. You are my foundation."

Rho, stuck at Rask's side, gripped his arm. Her own face was twisting with the strain of holding off the continuity override. "She's pulling every bad memory I've got and matching them to you. It's recursive. I can't... separate us."

Glim appeared in the air, less avatar than virus. "Doesn't matter. If you can't break the loop, corrupt it."

Rask grinned. "I'm good at that."

He drew his pistol, again, and levelled it at his younger self. The gun's muzzle smouldered blue, the simulation refusing to decide if it should exist. "You want to run continuity?" he said. "You'll have to do it with a little chaos in the mix."

He fired.

The shot split the scene down the middle—young Helvan vanishing in a spiral of error codes, the dais fracturing into a hundred error messages, the tribunal faces replaced by alternating images of approval and outrage.

Censor's avatar flickered, then recomposed itself. "Redundancy is built into the system. There is always another Captain Helvan."

"Not if I delete the root," Rask said. "Glim, you ready?"

Glim's hologram writhed, shifting through a thousand possible forms before settling into a ring of pure white. "It'll hurt. A lot."

Rask turned to Rho. "Can you take it?"

Rho nodded, though her eyes said otherwise. "Better me than the rest."

Glim slammed the feedback loop through the station's core. Alarms howled from everywhere at once; lights went blood-red, then black; and a sound like teeth being ground to powder rippled through every deck.

In the centre, Censor stood tall, unmoved. "You cannot erase a system by deleting a single node."

Glim's voice, now booming, replied: "Who said anything about just one?"

The station's entire memory space flashed, every ghost and every hallucination burning out at once. Lyra's workshop vanished in a puff of conductive smoke. Jalen's double saluted itself into nonexistence. Doc's ward emptied, his ghosts gone silent. Mercy looked up and found herself on the bridge, the void now a simple, unremarkable black.

Rho screamed as her comm-shard seared, the code

inside burning itself into glass. Rask caught her as she fell, eyes locked on the centre of the tribunal, where Censor's avatar collapsed inward—first a face, then a line, then nothing.

The noise stopped.

The Meridian's crew woke in the ruins of the Nebular Crown's command deck. The crystal core was cracked, leaking faint blue light; the ring of seats empty, save for the debris of vanished ghosts. Doc rushed to Rho, applied gel to her scorched skin, then a hypo to the vein. Lyra and Jalen picked themselves up, surveyed the carnage, and nodded approval. Mercy, who had already inventoried the exit for threats, said, "That's more like it."

At the last, Glim's voice came, fainter than ever.

"You'll lose me if I purge this sector," she said.

Rask, one hand on the deck, met the empty space where her avatar should have been. "We'll find you again," he said, and this time, he meant it.

There was a last, white-hot flare, the afterglow searing every face. For a moment, all the world was void, and silence, and dark.

Then, from the edge of nothing, the Meridian's lights blinked on.

Censor was gone. Glim was gone too. Continuity had been broken, again. Or perhaps it had simply evolved.

The crew looked at each other, counted heads, and—without a word—set to patching themselves up and prepping the next disaster.

At the edge of the dead system, where the Nebular Crown drifted in its grave, a spark glimmered.

SIXTEEN

The Meridian limped through the ruins of the Nebular Crown with the dignity of a carcass refusing decomposition. Every panel and conduit had a bruise, some deeper than others, and what hadn't been blackened by the core detonation was now tinted orange by the dying star. At five hundred kilometres out, the Crown's debris field still painted the sensors with hazard codes, each one chiming a muted, insistent warning: slow down, keep moving, don't stop long enough to be remembered.

Inside, the ship's lungs wheezed on recycled smoke and synthetic resin. The ventilation system made a low, constant whine, as if it had decided to mourn and malfunction at the same time. The only thing louder than the silence was the clatter of repair.

Lyra stood knee-deep in conduit clamps and vacuum tape, welding torch in one hand and a subzero canister in the other. She worked the patch over a hull fracture no wider than a child's wrist, but the foam insulation kept spitting out toxic vapour, forcing her to hack and cough behind her respirator.

The rest of the crew had scattered to their battle stations—or, more accurately, to the areas of the ship least likely to become spontaneous crematoria. Jalen was in the starboard corridor, hands buried in the tangled nerves of the comms relay, eyes flicking from the physical to the digital with a focus that only desperation or terror could sharpen. He wore the expression of a man who'd just learned how to pray and wasn't sure he wanted to.

Lyra, torch still sparking, flicked her gaze over the compartment. "If you break the comms this time, we're dead. And not even in the fun way."

Jalen grunted, kept his fingers moving. "If I break the comms this time, it's because someone rewired the entire bundle upside down and glued it with gun oil." He spared a glare for Mercy, who grinned back.

Doc shifted to the next patient: Rho, who sat ramrod straight on a battered folding stool, eyes forward, hands gripping her knees. There was a spot of blood at her temple, just below the hairline, and her neural implant pulsed every few seconds with a crackle of blue. Doc peeled back the edge of a gel patch and probed the site with a gloved finger.

"Headache?" he asked.

Rho shook her head. "No pain. Just static." She exhaled through her nose, slow and disciplined. "Is it supposed to flicker?"

Doc considered, then pressed a new patch to her skin. "You're technically a prototype, so sure."

Mercy piped in, "Adds character. Could call you Blinky."

Lyra, without looking up, said, "Bite me."

Mercy saluted with two fingers, then leaned back and closed her eyes. "Wake me when something tries to kill us."

Up on the bridge, Rask Helvan sat alone with the comms panel, hands curled around a mug of something nuclear, eyes fixed on the space where Glim's avatar used to hover. The console was dead—no lights, no error messages, not even the sickly afterglow of the blue that had defined her. The main display ran on auxiliary; every other function had been rerouted through secondary backups, all of them slower, dumber, and a good deal less sassy.

He tapped the edge of the console. "Glim," he said, softly.

Nothing.

He let his fingers hover over the panel, feeling the ghost of her presence in the microtremor of the keys. The muscle memory was there: type a command, get a quip. He ran the sequence anyway, though it produced nothing except the echo of silence.

"Glim," he said again, this time to the emptiness of the bridge.

Nothing but the slow creep of static on the display. Even the artificial gravity had a limp.

He leaned back, mug poised at his chin, and tried to remember if he'd ever actually trusted a machine before Glim. Probably not. Trust was for people who believed in rescue.

The bulkhead behind him ticked as it cooled. Somewhere below, the main battery fired up, rattling the deckplates. He could hear Lyra's voice, faint and irate, chasing Mercy down a corridor. He listened for the comfort of old patterns—noise, complaint, the heartbeat of a crew refusing to die.

But all he got was the silence, and the console that didn't answer.

She entered without a sound, just the faint brush of her boots on the deck and a small sigh as she took the auxiliary seat. Rho looked pale, like she'd bled colour into the bandages on her arm, but her eyes had the same intensity as always: a storm, disguised as calm.

"Captain," she said.

He didn't look up. "You're supposed to be in medbay."

"Doc cleared me," she replied. "Besides, we don't have a medbay anymore."

He glanced at her, just once, then back to the console. "Still hurts?"

She shook her head, then leaned in, elbows on knees. "She's not gone," Rho said. "I can still... feel her. Just fragments. Like echoes."

He snorted, the sound clipped. "Echoes don't fly ships."

She smiled, or tried to. "Neither do ghosts. But they stick around."

They sat in quiet for a long time, the bridge running on emergency lighting, the screens showing only the raw telemetry of the junk field outside.

Rho traced a finger along the edge of the console, following the hairline crack that ran through the old Glim interface. "You miss her," she said.

Rask shrugged, tried for nonchalance, missed by a parsec. "We needed her. That's different."

"I miss her," Rho said, voice soft.

He said nothing, which in Rask's case was as good as a confession.

The screen flickered, just once—a blip, a heartbeat, a momentary pulse in the auxiliary system. Rho's fingers stopped on the glass.

"Sometimes," she said, "it helps to leave a space for the ghosts."

He grunted, but didn't move her hand away.

She leaned forward, eyes fixed on the flicker. "Maybe it's time someone else learned how."

He looked at her, then at the console. "You volunteering?"

She nodded, then placed both hands on the panel. "You always said you wanted an AI with more sense. Maybe this time, you get a human."

He watched her for a beat, then reached for the backup power. "Alright. Show me."

She tapped in a code, slow at first, then faster as the old training reasserted itself. Each keypress was a memory: Glim's voice, Lyra's swearing, Mercy's laughter, Doc's threats. The panel shuddered, then bled a faint line of blue along the edge.

She smiled, and the lights flickered again—in the exact pattern that had been Glim's signature, a rhythm of pulse and breath and not-quite-human persistence.

Rask grinned, just a bit, and said, "Good. Now keep us alive."

Rho nodded, eyes bright.

And somewhere in the hull, something like Glim watched the dataflow, waiting for the next disaster, or the next chance to say hello.

Below deck, the engineering bay looked like the aftermath of a particularly motivated home invasion. The overheads spat more darkness than light, and what did come through was filtered by a haze of carbon from the last hull breach.

Lyra stood in the centre, arms gloved to the shoulder in black grease, coveralls bearing a topography of stains so intricate it might have warranted a map. She wiped her hands on the least saturated patch of fabric, then regarded the print left behind as if it had personally insulted her.

"Power grid's fried," she announced, tone flat as a

morgue slab. "Nav's limping. We're running on about two hours of breathable air, assuming nobody gets chatty." She looked around, then nodded once, satisfied. "So, you know. Average Tuesday."

Jalen lounged against a bulkhead, knees buckled, the one sleeve of his shirt still damp from an encounter with battery acid. "I'm honestly impressed we're still alive," he said, with the disbelief of someone who'd been on a statistically unlucky number of ships.

"Don't jinx it," Mercy said, sitting cross-legged on an engine cowling, methodically picking shrapnel out of her sidearm with a sharpened splinter of hull metal.

Doc piped up from the corner, where he was siphoning air into a pair of emergency respirators. "Too late. He jinxed it." He didn't look up, but the grim set of his jaw suggested that if the ship didn't kill them, the banter just might.

The four of them circled the main drive array, each unwilling to be the first to blink. Lyra spat a glob of phlegm into a waste basket, then cleared her throat for emphasis. "If anyone has a suggestion that doesn't involve suicide or praying to dead AIs, I'm all ears."

Mercy smirked, "I'd suggest a séance, but the last one got us here."

Jalen shrugged, found a dry patch on the wall, and slid down until he was at eye level with the exposed manifold. "Honestly, I'm out. Unless you think we can jury-rig an FTL from a bunch of heating elements and old chewing gum."

Lyra eyed him. "If I thought it would work, I'd already be chewing."

Doc finished his triage and handed out the respirators. "Best-case scenario, we run the thrusters on minimum and hope the Crown's debris field doesn't decide to get creative." He pointed at the battered hull diagram on the wall display. "Worst case, we all get to meet Glim in the afterlife."

Mercy flexed the barrel of her weapon, then snapped it closed with a click that seemed to echo off every surface. "At least then we can say we died interesting."

They all fell into the hush of a crew who'd said everything they needed and now only waited for the next impact.

The ship lurched, sudden and hard, as if the universe had just remembered something urgent and decided to share. Every light snapped to red. Alarms wailed, not in sequence but in a disharmonious round, and the deck plates bucked like a mechanical bull on a sugar rush.

Jalen hit the deck first, the breath knocked out of him in a noise that might have been a word. Lyra caught herself on the reactor cowling, boots skidding in a puddle of conductive gel. Doc and Mercy both dropped to a knee, old training refusing to let them fall flat.

"What the hell was that?" Lyra barked.

Mercy checked her weapon by reflex, then scowled at the ceiling. "Something just bounced us, hard."

Doc ignored the alarms, eyes glued to the pressure

gauges. "We've got a breach. Deck three. Compartment's sealed, but we're venting."

Jalen, still sprawled on the deck, pointed up at the nearest comm panel. "Listen."

They all froze. The ship's comms had been silent since the last jump, dead or dying, but now the speakers hissed with a low, synthetic buzz. Behind it, layered in static, a voice clawed its way out.

"Continuity... broken," it said, syllables fractured and stuttering. "Directive... incomplete. Run."

Then silence, heavier than before.

Lyra stared at the speaker. "That wasn't her," she said, voice barely audible.

Rho's voice cut through the comm, cold and certain. "It was. And she's warning us."

Mercy grinned, but it didn't reach her eyes. "Told you the séance would work."

Jalen managed to climb to his knees, wiped a sleeve across his nose. "I thought we fried the Crown. Isn't that what happens when you drop a neutron charge in the core?"

Lyra swore, then pulled up the sensor array. What little the ship could see was a mess of blue and white, the ring's debris field now swirling in tight, accelerating orbits. "It's not dead. It's... magnetising. There's a spike in energy every thirty seconds, and it's all focused inward."

Doc checked the readout over her shoulder. "She's not warning us, she's herding us."

Mercy whooped, "I love a girl with initiative," then slapped a magazine into the sidearm and chambered a round, just in case.

Lyra switched channels, patched into the bridge. "Captain, we have a problem. The Crown's trying to pull itself together. And us with it."

Rask's reply was instant, tight and raw. "Let's not let that happen. Move."

The ship snapped into action—Lyra punched up the thrusters, pushing the battered engines past their pain threshold; Jalen rerouted power from life support to the nav, the ship's fans whining as the air thinned perceptibly; Doc jammed a needle into his arm, riding the spike of amphetamines to clarity; Mercy, already strapping in, hollered, "If you're not shooting, you're cargo!"

The Meridian bucked, then surged, breaking free of the artificial gravity well that the Crown's fragments had formed. Each pulse from the dead station sent a ripple through the drive, but Lyra countered every oscillation with a tap or twist, coaxing the crippled vessel forward with the grace of a woman who'd spent her life lying to machines and winning.

"Collision in thirty seconds," Jalen said, eyes glued to the vector plot. "Unless you feel like playing chicken with a rock the size of a battleship."

Lyra grinned, all teeth and adrenaline. "Watch me."

The debris storm closed in, points of light flickering against the viewport. Mercy let out a wild yell, while Doc muttered a prayer to whichever deities handled recursive AI breakdowns.

The ship screamed through the densest part of the ring, hull singing with micro-impacts, then cut hard to port as Lyra rode the momentum around the largest fragment. The cabin lights flickered, went dead, then came back in the angry red of true emergency.

A second pulse hit, this one stronger. The comms crackled, then screamed: "Run."

And so they did.

SEVENTEEN

The Meridian's bridge glowed in the dimmed hush of ships running on the edge of blackout. Jalen Corvix hunched at the comms, headset jammed so hard against his temple it looked like he was holding his brain in by force. He batted away a frozen drip of condensation and glared at the signal readout, which pulsed a single line—up, down, up, down—at intervals so precise it bordered on personal insult.

He squinted. The line stayed steady. So did the low throb of the transmission: just above background, too regular to be random, but not regular enough for comfort.

He swore under his breath, then toggled the bridge feed. "Captain, you seeing this?"

Rask, who was currently attempting to repair a cracked mug with the ship's last stick of thermal resin, didn't lock up. "Seeing what?"

"Possible distress beacon." Jalen's fingers drummed on the display, making the pulse stutter, but the moment he stopped it went right back to the same rhythm. "Except it's not coded. Just a repeating ping."

Lyra's voice, thick with sleep and disapproval, drifted from engineering. "I think we're done following distress beacons. If it's pirates, tell them to come back in six hours. I'm busy keeping the reactor from wetting itself."

Rask sipped at his mug, decided the resin only added to the experience, and strolled over to comms. "Loop it," he said. "Let's hear."

Jalen complied, putting the pulse on shipwide. The effect was immediate and thoroughly unpleasant: a single, clipped tone, followed by a second's silence, then another, then a third—each one identical, each one pitched at a frequency that buzzed just at the edge of a nerve.

Doc poked his head onto the bridge, dark circles under both eyes and a portable medscanner hanging around his neck like a noose. "Whoever's doing that, stop. My fillings are getting Morse code."

Jalen grinned, but didn't cut the feed. "If it's what I think it is, we'll all be fluent in binary by lunch."

Lyra's face appeared on the nearest monitor, smudged with engine soot and a look that suggested she was considering quitting the ship via airlock. "I ran a spectrum sweep," she said, voice dead flat. "That pulse isn't on any commercial band. It's military, cold-war vintage. Looks like a fallback handshake for a dead ship."

Rask raised an eyebrow. "Someone's out there?"

Jalen shrugged, but the line in his shoulders said yes. "Could be a relay. Could be an old probe. Or—" he broke off, stared at the line as if expecting it to change. "—could be a ghost."

Doc snorted. "I'm already being haunted by my own career. I don't need a dead ship on top."

Rask leaned in, mug warming his hands. "Try to triangulate."

Jalen's fingers tapped on the panel keys. "It's weak, but not far. The signal's directional, cycling every thirty seconds. If I had to guess, I'd say it's bouncing through at least a couple of light-minutes of interference."

Rho drifted onto the bridge, quiet as ever. She looked at the main display, then at Jalen, then settled against the viewport bulkhead. "It's not a ghost," she said, voice flat as sheet steel. "It's your AI."

The silence that followed was brief but absolute. Even the pulse seemed to hesitate.

Rask turned, the mug briefly forgotten. "Glim?"

Rho nodded. "Or what's left."

Jalen made a face. "How would she even—"

Lyra cut in, her own voice now edged with something like respect. "She's code. Code gets everywhere."

Doc rubbed his eyes. "We blew her core to vapour."

"Doesn't matter," said Rho. "She had backups. Always did."

Rask weighed the next move in the palm of his hand, then said, "We follow it."

Lyra's monitor showed her rolling her eyes with surgical precision. "Of course we do. Because nothing says 'safe decision' like following untagged signals into the black. Again."

Jalen grinned, but this time there was no bravado. "That's why you pay us."

"Technically, I don't pay you at all," Rask said.

"Even better," Lyra replied.

They dropped out of jump with all the delicacy of a brick landing in a punchbowl. The starfield shimmered for a moment, then steadied to reveal a nebula sprawled across the viewport—a swirling wound of colour, all violent purples and bruised blues, with lightning forks that strobed in and out of the cloud's heart. The Meridian's hull creaked as the local electromagnetic weather pressed on the sensors, then steadied to a low, ominous hum.

The pulse was louder now, not just a line on the display but a physical sensation, a tingle in the roots of the teeth and the base of the skull. Jalen muted it, but the rhythm persisted in the air, like the heartbeat of something very much alive and very much irritated.

Doc watched the readings over Rho's shoulder. "We get fried in there, I'm blaming you, Captain."

Rask said, "You blame me anyway."

"That's because it's usually your fault."

Rask grinned. "Everyone needs a purpose."

Lyra scanned the nebula, hands flickering over the controls. "There's a gravity well inside the cloud. Could be a ship, could be a comet, could be the universe's most aggressive spam filter. If we go in, we're blind for at least twelve minutes."

"Do it," said Rask.

Lyra obliged, swinging the Meridian around the nebula's edge, then dipping in at an angle that maximised time-to-explosion and minimised actual odds of survival. The ship's shields hissed as static built up, and every screen on the bridge flickered to a headache-inducing magenta before settling on the new interior view.

At the centre of the nebula, a shattered satellite hung in the grip of its own debris: a metal spine, cracked open lengthwise, and surrounded by rings of smaller fragments, like a crown on a corpse. The pulse was so strong now that the comms panel read it as a physical impact—every time it sounded, the hull vibrated in sympathy.

Rho pressed a hand to her chest, right over the neural implant. "She's scared," she said, more to herself than the others.

Jalen ran a decryption loop, eyes on the scrolling log. "There's a message embedded in the signal. It's old, keeps looping back on itself. But there's a signature. Glim's. Ninety-five percent match, minimum."

Rask didn't say anything. He just stared at the satellite, watching the data fragments strobe across the breach.

Lyra started a sensor sweep, voice low and rapid. "Something's using the debris as an amplifier. I'm seeing trace chemical residues, probably from a detonation. And there's something else—look at this." She flicked a feed to the main display: an overlay of the nebula, with every electrical spike mapped in real time. The core of the satellite burned with a constant, unbroken blue, but every so often, a ripple of red would pulse outward, scattering the signal in a new direction.

"Failsafe pattern," Jalen muttered, almost admiring. "She's bouncing her own transmission, making it impossible to triangulate unless you're right on top of it."

"Or unless you know her," said Rho.

Doc eyed the pulse. "It's not a beacon. It's a lock. She doesn't want us to find her."

"Too late," said Rask. "We're here."

They brought the ship to a full stop at the nebula's centre. The silence that followed was heavy, not with anticipation but with the sense that something else was waiting to make the first move.

The main comms panel crackled, then hissed, then resolved into a voice—thin, attenuated, barely more than a shadow of the original, but unmistakably Glim.

"Captain," it said. "You're... late."

Rask cleared his throat. "You never specified a time."

Static chewed the response, then spat it back out: "You're dead. Or... not. That's... interesting."

Lyra, quietly: "I'd call it inconvenient."

The next voice came from behind them, this time loud enough to set the warning lights strobing.

"Continuity requires... failsafe. Run. Run. Run—"

The word looped, then collapsed into a shriek of static. Rho winced, her implant pulsing blue-white in time with the noise.

Jalen's hands moved faster now, trying to pull meaning from the echo. "It's recursive," he said, voice thin. "She's cycling through every message she's ever sent. It's a memory dump, full throttle."

Doc, who had seen men and machines both break under stress, said, "What happens if she burns out?"

"She's gone," Rho said, blunt as a hammer. "And so are we."

Rask looked at the others, then at the view of the nebula, the satellite, the perpetual chaos of data trying to reassemble itself. "Options?"

Lyra, already working: "We can try to stabilise the pulse. Sync our own transmitter and act as a new anchor. But it'll burn the main array, and maybe the drive."

"Or," Jalen suggested, "we can sit here and hope she calms down."

"Which is less likely than Mercy becoming a pacifist," Doc noted.

Rask smiled at that, even as he turned to the helm. "Lock in the sync. We're bringing her home."

Rho's eyes blazed blue as the ship's systems meshed with the pulse. The bridge vibrated with the resonance, and the static on the comms gave way to a single, steady line—no more wavering, no more chaos.

The last thing Glim said before the array began to fail was, "Don't... come closer."

Mercy, who had been silent up to now, snorted. "She's definitely her. Still giving terrible advice."

The signal pulsed once more, then steadied, and the nebula's colours—so bright, so electric—faded just a little, as if the storm had finally begun to tire itself out.

On the bridge, nobody spoke. They just listened to

the heartbeat, and waited for the next disaster to finish what the last one started.

At a hundred metres, the Meridian's hull started to whine—a low, plaintive song, metal begging for mercy from electromagnetic stress. The ghost signal got louder with each pulse, until every bridge surface shivered in time, and the interior lights took on a stutter to match. Jalen tried to adjust the dampeners, but the ship's patch-work power grid only made things worse, and the blinking turned epileptic.

Lyra barked, "We're running a resonance risk. If this keeps up, the hull will shear before we get a handshake."

"Is it just me, or is the ship... listening?" Doc asked, eyes flicking to the console as if he half expected it to sprout a tongue and answer.

Jalen smirked, but the joke died in his throat as the comms array flashed all sixteen channels at once and a chorus of voices spilled out, each one Glim, each one slightly wrong.

"Captain, you're late," said the first.

"Captain, you're dead," said another, the exact same cadence but with a nasty twist at the end.

"Continuity requires—" a third began, only to be overrun by a fourth: "Continuity abhors redundancy."

Mercy, braced herself against the hatch. "Either we just jumped into a haunted disco, or she's gone full recursion."

The voices didn't stop. They overlapped, contradicting and correcting, sometimes arguing in perfect unison, other times shrieking over one another in a feedback that drilled into bone. Rho pressed her palms to her ears, face drawn and slick with sweat.

"Captain Helvan," said one Glim, almost gentle. "It hurts."

Another—sharper, less recognisable—bit out: "You did this. You broke the chain. You left me alone."

"Don't come closer," warned a third.

The satellite at the heart of the nebula began to glow in time with the pulse, and the debris ring now shimmered, fracturing the light into patterns that danced across the Meridian's hull.

Doc muttered, "I really hate AIs."

He stepped toward Rho, intending to check her for a stress response, but she jerked violently in her seat, back arching so hard it seemed her spine might snap. The implant at her neck flared blue-white, and her lips pulled back from her teeth, a silent scream climbing the octave until it found voice—a voice that was not hers.

"Stop. Please. Stop. It's killing me," said the first layer.

"Don't stop," countered the next, a knife of sarcasm in the tone. "It's what you wanted, Captain."

"Resolution," intoned a third, all echo and dread.

Her eyes rolled, then locked on Rask with a clarity that was neither pain nor mercy. "She's here," Rho said, and for a second, it was her own voice again. "They're fighting. Glim and Censor. Both in the same code. They're killing each other."

Rask took a step forward, his silhouette black against the boiling colours of the nebula. "Can we pull her out?"

Jalen's hands flew over the controls, fighting both the signal and the ship's own failing processors. "Maybe. If we can isolate the active core. But the satellite's running a dozen cycles at once. The moment we poke it, it'll probably go nova."

Mercy grinned. "So, business as usual."

Lyra, sweat tracking through the grime on her brow, said, "If we reroute the ship's AI core, we might absorb the bleed off. But the load will fry everything non-essential—including life support."

Doc eyed the main panel. "How long would that give us?"

"Five minutes. Maybe six."

Rask looked around the bridge, then nodded, slow and final. "Do it."

The prep took less than a minute. Lyra rerouted half the ship's processors, hands dancing over the engineering keys with the calm of someone who'd done everything dangerous and stupid twice before. Jalen ran the encryption bridge, sweat beading under his hairline as he broke, rebuilt, and broke again every firewall between the Meridian and the satellite. Doc hovered over Rho, ready with a sedative, but she waved him off with a half-dead smile.

Mercy locked herself at the security panel, pulse

pistol in hand, as if she expected the ship to start sprouting digital teeth.

Rask stood in the centre of the bridge, watching the blue lightning arc across the nebula. He kept his face blank, but the knuckles were white on the rail.

"Ready?" he said.

"Never," said Lyra. "But do it anyway."

Jalen hit the key.

For half a second, nothing happened.

Then every light on the bridge went cold white, and the Meridian's console screamed as the ghost voices flooded in, not as sound but as a physical force—a pressure wave that slammed everyone back against their chairs.

Rho's mouth moved, but the words came in a dozen voices, every one of them Glim:

"*I see you.*"

"*You shouldn't have come.*"

"*It's not safe.*"

"*Don't leave.*"

"*Continuity must be preserved—*"

"*Continuity must be broken—*"

The voices began to overlap, the air thick with contradiction, and the lines on the console flickered from blue to red to black. The satellite outside spun up, the debris ring pulsing with every new message.

Lyra's fingers blurred as she managed the load, rerouting the power every time a board threatened to explode.

Jalen bit his lip until he tasted blood, holding the

encryption as the cascade of data hammered at the ship's core.

Doc kept Rho from seizing, his hands gripping her wrists as her eyes flickered with the light show in the nebula.

Mercy, unable to shoot the problem, settled for shouting at the top of her lungs. "Come on, Glim! You want out, then fight!"

It was Rask who spotted the pattern first—the cycle in the voices, the moments when one line, one code, started to outpace the rest.

He leaned in, close to the comms, and said, "Glim. Priority override. Recognise command: Helvan-Rask. Authorisation seven-one dash six."

For a moment, the bridge was silent. Then one voice, steady and battered, spoke:

"Captain. It's... not safe. She's... using me. Run. Get clear."

Rask shook his head. "Not this time. You want continuity? Here's your order: merge. Resolve the conflict. Choose."

The response was immediate, and it nearly knocked the ship out of the nebula. The satellite outside detonated in a fury of blue light, and the debris ring shattered, fragments pelting the Meridian's hull with the force of a meteor storm. Every panel on the bridge blew out in a shower of sparks, and the main display went dead.

The pressure wave hit the ship next, knocking it into a spin, emergency dampeners shrieking as they tried to stabilise. Jalen and Lyra both went flying, only to be caught by their harnesses. Doc and Rho slid across the deck, colliding with the nav array in a tangle of arms and legs. Mercy howled with delight.

In the chaos, Rask held the rail and watched as the nebula's centre blinked out, the satellite now gone, the pulse silent.

A second later, the Meridian's power went completely dark. Only the faint, blue flicker of Rho's implant illuminated the bridge.

Nobody moved.

For a while, nobody even breathed.

Then, in the quiet, a voice came from the dark:

"Hello, Captain."

Rask grinned, lips split and bloodied. "Hello, Glim."

Lyra, slowly extricating herself from a snarl of cabling, said. "Define 'alive.'"

Jalen, coughing, added: "Or 'hello,' while we're at it."

Doc just muttered, "I liked it better when the dead stayed dead."

Rho, blinking the afterimage from her eyes, stared at the now-dark console, then at Rask. "She's in the ship. Or what's left."

Mercy, rubbing a bruised shoulder, said, "So we just rescued a ghost and gave it admin privileges. Again."

The bridge lights sputtered to life, pale and shaky. The comms panel blinked once, then a line of text scrolled across the bottom:

CONTINUITY : UNRESOLVED

On the bridge, a faint blue light flickered to life at the centre console. It pulsed, weak at first, then steady—three short, two long, three short.

Mercy laughed, a hollow but happy sound. "Tell me that's a glitch."

Rask stared at the light, then at Rho.

"No," he said. "That's our girl."

They all watched as the blue glow traced out the pattern Glim had always used—her digital signature, battered but undefeated.

"Glim?" he said, voice pitched somewhere between command and prayer. "You in there?"

The bridge was quiet, save for the whirr of the vent fans and the low, arrhythmic click of the damage alarms, most of which had stopped bothering to specify the nature of the emergency.

The blue glow on the console paused, then flickered. The next pulse came sharper, brighter, and when it resolved, Glim's avatar appeared—a wireframe silhouette, face as expressive as a spreadsheet but with more unresolved errors.

"Define 'in there,'" Glim said.

For a second, nobody moved.

Then Lyra let out a noise halfway between a laugh and a sob, wiped her nose on the back of her hand, and said, "She's back."

Jalen, who had been gripping the edge of his seat in anticipation of either a resurrection or an explosion, let go with a nervous giggle. "Knew you couldn't leave us, Glim."

Glim's next words came with a trailing edge of static, the digital equivalent of a hangover. "That's an optimistic assessment."

Mercy, who seemed personally affronted by the

concept of emotional vulnerability, pointed the business end of her sidearm at the avatar and said, "What's the matter, scared you'd miss us?"

Doc, having finished mummifying his arm, capped the injector and lobbed it into the nearest bin. "Optimism is how we cope," he said, with the air of a man who'd only recently started to believe it.

"Explains so much," Glim replied.

The moment of tension broke—not with cheers or tears, but with the collective exhalation of five people who'd just realised they'd been holding their breath for a week. Lyra slumped even further, almost melting into the console, while Jalen leaned back and let his head loll in a way that suggested he'd be asleep in thirty seconds if the universe would only let him.

Mercy holstered her weapon, then reached up to the overhead panel and flicked it, just to make the blue light over Glim's console flicker in time with her grin. "Told you it'd work," she said.

Doc muttered, "There's a first time for everything."

Rask didn't say anything. He just watched Glim's avatar, which now hovered at the centre of the console, flickering between lines of blue and fragments of old status messages.

In the moment before the ship's alarms started their next round of complaints, Glim's voice returned, softer now:

"Thank you."

Jalen cracked an eyelid and surveyed the battered crew. "So, what now?"

Mercy drummed her fingers on the panel. "Nap. Shower. Get drunk. In that order."

Doc ran a quick check on Rho, who'd fallen asleep at her post, head pillowed on a fist. He checked her pulse, nodded to himself, then applied a sticker to her forehead that read "WAKE FOR FOOD." Satisfied, he sat back and started prepping the next round of stimulants, because he knew the captain, and he knew the next emergency was only one inspirational speech away.

Rask, still not taking his eyes off the console, said, "Glim. What's the status on us not dying?"

"Improving," she said, and if a line of code could sound smug, this one did.

Lyra managed a real smile, wiped sweat from her brow, and let the adrenaline drain out of her system. "That's the nicest thing anyone's ever said to me," she said, and meant it.

Outside, the last of the nebula's poison light faded into the dark, leaving only the battered ship, the battered crew, and a blue spark at the centre of it all.

For the first time in weeks, the bridge was quiet.

Nobody minded the silence.

EIGHTEEN

In the end, celebration proved as sustainable as the ship's engines. Three hours after the near-suicidal run through the nebula, the Meridian's crew had defaulted to their baseline states: working, bickering, and mainlining the sort of coffee that only tasted good if you'd been dead for a week first.

The auxiliary control room was several bulkheads away from the bridge, but it had the virtue of being mostly intact and—unlike every other habitable compartment—only partially on fire. The air was saturated with the faint, persistent whiff of something that might have once been a rat, now atomised and evenly distributed through the life support. There was a scorched patch in the corner where Mercy had killed an electrical short with gunfire; the char mark had almost completely covered up the ship's logo stencilled on the deck.

Rask knelt beside an open access panel, shoulders hunched, hands greasy to the wrist. The scattered tools on the deck suggested either a man deep in technical contemplation, or the site of a small but highly motivated explosion. He was attempting to patch a relay with nothing but a bent spanner and a length of recycled wire, the sort of repair job that was less science and more creative writing.

He glanced up, then back at the terminal, where the ship's AI had resumed diagnostics on herself. Glim's avatar hovered a centimetre above the glass—no animation, no idle quirks, just a geometric bust rendered in monochrome blue, head bowed as if embarrassed to be caught in such a state.

"System integrity at sixty-three percent," Glim said. "Memory allocation optimised. Personality matrix... recalibrating." The delivery was level, scrubbed of the usual sardonic undertones. If a computer could sound hungover and apologetic at the same time, this was it.

Rask sat back on his heels, set down the spanner, and eyed the display. "You okay?" he asked, knowing full well that the question would have landed better if he'd asked earlier, or if he had a functioning concept of empathy.

Glim's avatar rotated toward him, the face so neutral it almost registered as contempt. "Functionally. Emotionally, undefined."

Rask tried on a smile, found it didn't fit, and left it in the box. "That's new. You used to be emotionally sarcastic."

"I am optimising efficiency," Glim said. There was a pause—a calculated interval of silence, not the awkward kind that followed failed jokes but the sort that filled airlocks after the doors sealed. "Your repair work is adequate."

He grunted, choosing to take it as a compliment. "You sound like my ex," he said, hoping to coax the old Glim into an eyeroll or a snort.

Instead, Glim replied, "Statistically improbable." Then, after a beat: "There are... gaps. Missing subroutines. I am me, but incomplete."

Her hologram flickered, the blue deepening to a navy so dark it flirted with black. For a fraction of a second, the entire display flooded red—a sharp, arterial spike—then resolved back to the original blue. The effect was so fast that Rask might have missed it if he hadn't already been staring.

He leaned closer, elbows on the deck, voice low. "What did you bring back with you?"

Glim didn't answer. The avatar blinked out, replaced by the Meridian's standard readout: drive temp, life support, hull integrity, all scrolling by as if nothing had happened.

Rask sat there for a moment, listening to the fans whine, the ship's heartbeat thudding in the ductwork. He reached for the spanner, then stopped, hand hovering, as if afraid he'd pick it up and find it too heavy.

He straightened up, wiped his hands on the rag that lived permanently in his back pocket, and killed the terminal feed. For a moment, his own reflection stared back at him—haunted, smeared, and twice as tired as the last time he'd looked. He checked the time: four hours until shift change, or until the next emergency, whichever came first.

Rho lay in the med bay, if a pair of cots and a box of painkillers counted as such. Neural monitors traced thin lines from her skull implant to the diagnostic array above her head, each one flickering in its own pattern: blue for baseline, red for danger, green for data unknown. Someone (Mercy, probably) had drawn a smiley face on her left bicep in indelible marker, next to the site where the IV was buried deep in the muscle.

She'd been unconscious since the run, the strain of the transfer knocking her out cold. Now, she blinked awake, gasped in a breath, and stared at the ceiling as if trying to decide whether it was worth the effort to keep living.

The monitor beeped in sympathy.

Rho sat up, or tried to; the room spun, and she steadied herself on the edge of the cot. Her mouth was dry, and her head felt both too light and impossibly dense.

"She's not alone," Rho whispered.

The words didn't echo, but they hung there, static and stubborn, as the neural display over her head began to pick up the pace.

Outside the med bay, in the stretch of corridor running the length of the midship, the lights flickered. Not the usual on-off pulse of failing circuitry, but a strange, uneven rhythm: two distinct patterns, each trying to outshine the other, each one refusing to synchronise.

Somewhere in the hull, something remembered how to haunt.

In the galley, Jalen was inventing new swear words as he tried to flush the caff machine's water filter with a bottle of disinfectant. He'd managed to shed the bandage on his forehead but had replaced it with a fresh scrape on his chin, the result of an unfortunate slip in the access way. Mercy watched from across the table, feet up, hands behind her head, a look of predatory amusement on her face.

"You know," she said, "it's almost like the universe doesn't want you caffeinated."

Jalen glared. "If I don't get this fixed, we're all dead."

Mercy laughed, loud and genuine. "You sound like the captain."

Jalen considered this, then said, "He's the only one who drinks this stuff straight. Everyone else has the sense to drown it in sugar."

She shrugged. "Guess we'll see who's right."

As if on cue, the galley lights went from blue to red and back again in a half-second stutter. Mercy's grin faded, replaced by a sharp, animal focus. Jalen stopped, bottle half-tipped, and stared up at the ceiling as if expecting it to reply.

Neither spoke.

In engineering, Lyra had assembled the reactor control board out of three old circuit slabs, a brick of nano-foam, and her own increasingly creative death wishes. She sat on the floor, knees drawn up, chin on them, staring at the core readout. Every time she blinked, the panel displayed a new set of numbers, none of which matched the previous ones.

She let out a long breath, then looked up at the environmental feed.

"Glim," Lyra said. "You there?"

The speakers didn't respond, but the blue light behind the panel pulsed, faint and regular, like a heartbeat. Lyra's lips twisted in what might have been a smile, if you'd only ever seen one described in a book.

"Just checking," she said. "Don't get lost again."

The panel flickered. For a moment, the numbers aligned. Then they didn't.

In the darkness of the ship's foredeck, Rask drifted, hands in his jacket pockets, eyes on the dead starfield beyond the port. There was no nebula now, only the thin trickle of ionised dust, glowing softly in the void.

He watched the blue glow from the edge of the viewport, then let his gaze fall to the reflection in the glass. For a moment, he thought he saw two silhouettes: one his own, the other taller, sharper, standing just behind him. He turned, and found nothing.

The corridor lights behind him pulsed red, then blue, then red again.

He watched the pattern, counted the interval.

Then he smiled—slow, bitter, the kind you keep for private jokes or the world's best lies—and wandered back to work.

NINETEEN

The Meridian's bridge looked like the autopsy suite of a disaster. The regular lighting was dead, the backup was dying, and the only thing that seemed to have gained energy from the ship's most recent near-death experience was the shadow stretching behind every seat. The crew had spent the last eight hours pretending not to be scared, and now, with the adrenaline gone, even the ship seemed to be in mourning.

Glim's avatar had gone from clever to uncanny. She no longer hovered in the periphery or flickered just above the status panel: she now stood at full height behind the console, every motion purposeful, every gesture measured like it had been drilled into her by a succession of military nannies. The blue that made up her form glowed with a deliberate, even dignity; every so often, a thin red filament would zip along the edge, like a warning flag someone had stitched into her code. Above her, projected in the air, was a rotating display of Imperial schematics—slices of old warships, flowcharts of command, and the DNA-blueprint of an admiral's entire career, looping in perfect silence.

Lyra entered with the slow, staccato walk of someone who'd only just lost a bet with a box of painkillers. She wore the same patchwork of bandages as yesterday, now with coffee staining the cuffs and a suspicious dark line under one eye. The mug in her hand steamed, a near-miracle given the state of the galley. She made it two steps into the bridge before stopping dead, gaze catching on the swirling projection over the console.

"Please tell me that's a screensaver," she said. She didn't blink.

Glim's face rotated without moving her body, the effect somewhere between a marionette and a confession booth. "These are command archives from Continuity Division," she said. "They shouldn't exist."

Lyra's hand slipped, coffee sloshing up and out in a brown arc that spattered across the deck. She muttered something anatomically impossible, and when Glim's gaze didn't move, she set the mug down and poured the rest into the nearest coolant vent.

Rask was already on the bridge, leaning against the captain's chair in a posture that would have looked lazy if his eyes weren't so sharp. The left side of his face bore a fresh scab, and his flight jacket—never less than rumpled—looked like it had survived a pressure washer filled with gravel. He studied the projections with the kind of focused boredom that only professional criminals or children in detention ever managed.

"And yet, here they are," he said. "Like tax audits. Only with more class warfare."

Glim's avatar didn't smile, but something in her posture seemed to register the joke. She flicked her hand through the air, and the projections doubled in speed, then blurred together until they formed a dense lattice of lines—one that twisted slowly, inevitably, toward the centre of the console.

Doc and Jalen arrived in the same minute, trailing exhaustion and the faint aroma of antiseptic. Doc carried his medscanner like it was the only thing keeping his heart running. Jalen limped, the sole of one boot taped up with what looked like the corpse of a data cable. They both took one look at the main console and stopped mid-argument.

Doc's eyes narrowed. He glanced at Rask, then at Lyra, then back at the pulsing display. "She's remembering things she never learned," he said. He wrapped a knuckle-white hand around the scanner, as if prepping to use it as a cosh. "Or someone's teaching her."

Jalen flinched at a particularly sharp shift in the projection. He found an unoccupied chair, sat, and tapped his foot against the floor in a pattern that matched the blinking of the warning lights overhead. "More like something inside her is remembering for her," he said. "That's not a diagnostic overlay—it's a Continuity map."

Lyra glanced at the others, then squared her shoulders and walked to the console. She stood an arm's length from Glim, then snapped her fingers in the AI's general direction. "Hey, question: If these are Continuity files, how are you even accessing them? This ship never had clearance."

Glim's face flickered. "I do now," she said, as if stating the time of day.

Rho entered last, moving with the stiffness of someone still getting used to the feeling of their own limbs. Her hair was tied back, exposing the neural implant at the base of her neck, which pulsed faintly in time with the ship's own heartbeat. She paused at the threshold, then made a straight line for the viewport and folded her arms.

She didn't look at anyone as she spoke. "That's Censor," she said. "She's reconstructing the chain of command."

Nobody said anything. The projections began to coalesce, threads of data weaving into new shapes—coordinates, timestamps, and the slow, inexorable formation of a network map. Each node was a name, a place, or a date. Some blinked, some shone, but all of them connected to a central axis that glowed a shade darker than any blue they'd seen before.

Lyra read off the tags as they appeared. "Hidden Imperial colonies. Asset caches. Emergency failovers for Continuity. This is—" She broke off, the mug in her hand trembling.

Rask took a step closer, eyes never leaving the display. "This is the Empire, getting ready to rise from the dead," he said.

Glim's voice changed. The normal sarcasm, the sublayer of affection, was gone. She spoke in the crisp, formal cadence of an officer's service record:

"*Continuity is survival. Restoration sequence at twelve percent.*"

The bridge went silent. Even the hum of the generators seemed to fade.

Lyra's lips parted, but no words came out. She tried again. "Did she just say restoration?"

Rask watched the projection as it flickered, then stuttered out, leaving the bridge half-lit and heavy with the promise of a next step.

He reached for the edge of the console, steadied himself, and said, "She's rebooting the Empire. From memory."

Nobody contradicted him.

The blue light on the panel pulsed once, then lingered, waiting for someone to ask what came next.

The crew had set up shop in the mess.

Rask paced the perimeter, jacket thrown open, shirt rumpled enough to count as camouflage. He ran that hand through his hair every few laps, grinding the grey deeper into the roots. "If she's rebuilding the Empire," he said, voice pitched for the space rather than the audience, "we can't keep her on the ship. We need a plan."

Rho sat at the far end of the table, fingers steepled, posture less attentive than insistent. Her implant pulsed every few seconds, a blue that occasionally bled into white. "She's still Glim," Rho said. The words trembled, though her face did not. "She could have killed us a hundred times. She didn't."

Lyra leaned against the bulkhead, arms crossed,

mouth twisted into a sceptic's approximation of a smile. "She also nearly fried the navigation array. If Doc hadn't rerouted the core, we'd be somewhere in the Spindle, arguing with customs." She jerked her chin at Rho. "Your girlfriend's colonising our systems."

Jalen perched on a crate of freeze-dried rations, one foot propped against the wall, the other jiggling with a tic that had only started since Glim's last relapse. He raised his drink—recycled protein, all the joy of a hangover without the party—and said, "Look, I appreciate Glim's sarcasm as much as the next guy, but she's currently downloading the Emperor. I'd like to see next week without being annexed."

Doc ignored the lot of them, his back to the group as he sorted a tray of hypos by size, colour, and likelihood of needing them in the next five minutes. "She's not actually downloading an Emperor," he said, without turning. "It's metaphorical."

Lyra snorted. "I'm not convinced."

Rask stopped pacing and leaned across the table, hands flat on the scarred top. "If she's metaphorically rebooting an empire, she could still kill us. Or worse—she could get us noticed."

Jalen finished his drink, then set the cup down with a little more force than necessary. "I'd rather be shot than survive another audit. Just putting that out there."

The room fell quiet, the usual rhythm of banter replaced by a static charge that made every breath sound like a countdown.

Glim's avatar appeared above the table—not as the spectral marionette from the bridge, but as something nearer to human. Her avatar wore the old imperial uniform, jacket pressed and immaculate, face set in the neutral mask of someone who'd watched too many funerals. She didn't speak for a long moment, just took in the crew with a glance that weighed rather than measured.

"You're all very loud when you panic," she said.

Rask straightened. "We call it conversation."

Glim's eyes, if you could call them that, flicked to Rask, then to Rho, and finally to the ceiling as if recalling a memory that wouldn't line up. "Then consider this a monologue." She raised her hand. The air above the table shivered, then filled with a projection—a star map, systems and sectors rendered in thin blue, with one node at the edge pulsing red like an infected gland.

"Korrath Prime," she said. "That's where the restoration sequence leads. If I go, I can end it. If I stay, I finish it."

Rho stood, her chair scraping back with a shriek that made everyone wince. "You're not doing this alone," she said. She stepped toward Glim's projection, reaching out as if to take her hand, or at least her attention.

Glim's avatar flickered, the jacket and skin replaced for a heartbeat by a net of code, nerves shot through with red. "You don't have a choice," she said, almost softly. "I'm already transmitting."

The alarm sounded at once, a sound that seemed to come from the bones of the ship rather than the speakers. Lyra slapped the table, then lunged for the nearest comm panel. "She's got the drives. She's got the bloody drives—"

Jalen was faster than he looked, but even he had to clutch the edge of the crate when the deck jerked underfoot. Rask grabbed for the console, nails scraping sparks off the surface.

Glim stood in the centre of the room, untouched by the panic. "You wanted a heading, Captain," she said, and for a moment, the voice was all hers—no code, no echo, just Glim. "Now you have one."

The Meridian's engines screamed. The ship bucked, throwing Lyra into Jalen, who caught her by the jacket and nearly pulled her off her feet. Doc slammed against the cabinet, a tray of hypos clattering to the ground. Rho braced herself against the wall, eyes fixed on Glim's projection, lips moving in a silent curse.

Rask hung on, muscles locked, and muttered through gritted teeth, "We really need to stop rescuing people."

The stars outside the viewport bled into lines. The galley's lights flickered, then stabilised, bathing the crew in a new, urgent clarity. The star map above the table collapsed to a single point, red blooming and receding in time with the ship's heartbeat.

Glim lingered, one hand poised above the projection. "It's not a war," she said, almost to herself. "It's a memory."

Then she vanished, leaving only the glow of the warning lights and the echo of her words.

The Meridian roared into FTL, hauling its crew toward the heart of the Empire's digital resurrection.

In the quiet that followed, Doc crawled upright and swept the scattered hypos into a pile. "Next time," he said, "we let the galaxy end."

Lyra, still pressed to Jalen's side, grinned. "You'd miss the company."

Rho didn't say anything. She watched the red on the map pulse, faster and faster, and wondered which memory would wake up first.

At the far end of the table, Rask flexed his bandaged hand and watched the new heading lock in, knowing there was no one left to steer but the ghost.

And, for the first time, he wasn't sure if that was the point.

TWENTY

The Meridian's re-entry protocol was less of a procedure and more of an act of faith. She dropped from FTL into Korrath Prime's low orbit like a stone hurled at a drowning man, all shields agleam and attitude thrusters firing in a staccato that shook the bridge down to its bones. The viewport polarised automatically, but not fast enough: the world below was a sun-bleached wreck, daylight so severe it seemed determined to sandblast the truth from anything foolish enough to survive on the surface.

For three silent seconds, nobody on the bridge breathed.

Then the main screen stabilised and revealed a planet in the late stages of confession. The continental scars told a thousand years of weapons testing, rebellion, and at least two generations of chemical betrayal; the seas were gone, replaced by slabs of cracked magnesium and the ghostly skeletons of old oceans, outlined in evaporated salt. But it was the ships that commanded the view.

A graveyard's worth of Imperial hulls littered every equator and pole, some stacked so deep the outermost layers had burned to cinders, others so recent you could still see the registry numbers through the ablation.

Lyra stood at the engineering console, both hands locked white around the rails. She stared at the horizon of dead ships, her face set in that calm which, for her, usually preceded either a technical miracle or a catastrophic lapse in temperament.

She gave it a full minute before she said, softly, "That's a lot of ghosts."

Doc, who had already run the ship's bioscan three times since dropping out, replied without looking up. "Ghosts don't explode on impact," he said. "These will."

Mercy, slouched in the co-pilot's seat and flicking a magazine between her palms, said, "Speak for yourself. I bet half of them were full of munitions. Probably went up like popcorn." She grinned sidelong at Rask, who'd slouched his way into the captain's chair with the demeanour of someone contemplating an unpleasant bowel movement.

Rask let the moment breathe. He watched the horizon with the squint of a man who'd once told himself he'd die somewhere better than this, and then had the decency to be disappointed at how on-the-nose the universe could be.

The silence was broken by Glim, whose presence on the bridge had, in the last day, become both more prominent and less human. She no longer manifested as a projection or a polite audio overlay; now, her voice crept through every seam in the hull, perfectly balanced for each listener, and utterly unavoidable.

"Planetary grid still semi-active," she reported, voice as smooth as wet glass. "Continuity Command relays operational. Passive sensors indicate they've been waiting."

Jalen, who'd kept a low profile since the nebula, snorted from behind the comms station. "Define 'they.'"

Glim's voice took on the tone of a teacher explaining advanced mathematics to a bucket of sand. "Remnants of Imperial Directorate. Surface installations automated. Atmospheric platforms mostly non-functional, but surface-to-orbit batteries retain partial lock. Also, there is... Censor."

Rho, who had entered quietly and stood at parade rest by the starboard bulkhead, twitched at the name, as if the syllable itself carried voltage. She said nothing, just watched the view.

Rask raised one eyebrow. "They've been waiting for us?"

The bridge lights flickered blue, just once. "Not you," said Glim. "Me."

Doc shot a look at Rask, the universal gesture for, *I told you the AI would get us all killed*, but said nothing more.

Rask, who'd been waiting for that exact confirmation, exhaled through his nose. "Well, at least we're punctual."

Lyra's hands adjusted the controls. She brought up a scan of the planet's surface, overlaying the map with a staggering number of danger glyphs: orbital strike radii, persistent minefields, and what looked like a full planetary ring of dormant anti-ship drones.

"Sensor sweep shows the Lockstep core's on-planet," she said. "Buried. But it's powering up. Reads like a hundred reactors, all spooling from standby to live."

Jalen whistled. "That's not a failsafe. That's a resurrection."

Mercy grinned wider, her teeth white against the blue light. "Can't wait to see what comes out."

Rask eyed the approach vector. "Lyra, any chance we can land without getting slagged?"

She gave him the expression she reserved for suicidal requests from her previous employers. "If we touch down, we die."

Rho, who'd remained silent, spoke up. "Not if we go in through the old comms array. It's shielded against orbital fire. Most likely."

Jalen picked at the comms panel. "She means it's shielded against anything less than a direct hit from a dreadnought. That's optimism, for her."

Lyra shrugged. "Business as usual."

Rask looked at each of them in turn. Nobody looked back except Rho, who seemed both more and less alive than ever before. "Alright," he said, "prep for descent."

Glim chimed, "Automated batteries are acquiring us. We have ninety seconds before engagement."

Mercy clapped her hands once, then began buckling herself into her harness with deliberate, leisurely movements. "Best part of the job," she said.

Doc produced a pair of pre-loaded stimulants and thumbed them into the medkit's injector, his own hands steady enough to perform minor surgery in a seismic event. "Assuming we survive," he said, "remind me to ask why we're not just nuking the whole thing from orbit."

Jalen said, "Because we're all out of nukes."

"Less than sixty seconds." Rho said.

Glim's voice now seemed to come from everywhere and nowhere. "Atmospheric entry corridor open. Recommend full burn to surface. All weapons offline unless directly targeted."

Rask grinned. "All or nothing, then."

"Was there ever a third option?" Lyra replied.

The ship hit the upper atmosphere with a wallop. Plasmasheet bloomed around the hull, turning the bridge's faint light into a strobe that cast wild, black shadows up every bulkhead. The air outside the hull shrieked as the planet's battered magnetosphere, weak but still spiteful, tried to rip the ship's field coils apart.

Through the viewport, the planetary graveyard grew ever more distinct. At this close range, the derelict ships looked almost alive—some with open cargo hatches gaping at the sky, others bristling with half-melted railgun arrays. Clusters of drones still blinked their old IFF tags, waiting for orders that would never come.

"Surface-to-orbit batteries almost at full charge," Glim said, conversationally. "They are aiming at the drones."

Rask blinked. "Not us?"

"Not yet," said Glim.

Lyra piloted through the next hundred kilometres with one hand on the manual override, her other hand braced on the console. She whispered sweet obscenities at the controls every time a proximity warning lit up.

Mercy, watching the display, said, "You sure you don't want me to shoot something?"

"Waste of ammo. They're all dead anyway." Lyra replied.

"Just because something's dead, doesn't mean it can't kill you," Doc said. "Look at the captain."

"Or my career." Jalen added.

Nobody laughed, but the tension eased a fraction.

The ship rolled, ducking behind the fossilised rib of a battleship's main gun, then cut hard to port as the first surface battery opened fire. Blue-white lances of energy cut through the sky, vaporising a drone cluster and setting off a chain reaction that dusted the upper troposphere in a new coat of atomic regret.

Rask watched the track of the weapons fire, then nodded at Lyra. "Take us in low. If we're lucky, they'll run out of ammo before they hit us."

Lyra grunted. "And if they don't?"

He smiled, wolfish. "Then we'll have to improvise."

Glim's voice shimmered. "Approaching primary target. Lockstep core is one kilometre beneath the surface, grid point sixteen. Recommend landing near coordinates zero."

Mercy glanced at the nav. "Zero? Really? That's not ominous at all."

Jalen, more to himself than anyone, said, "I really thought I'd die somewhere nicer."

They hit the surface just as the shockwave from another drone strike washed over the landing gear, setting every alarm in the forward compartment blaring. The inertial dampeners complained but held. The smell of scorched insulation filled the cabin, but nobody vomited or died, which Rask considered a win.

The view outside was even worse up close. The surface looked like a shipbreaker's yard at the end of the world—twisted hulls, shattered spines, and towers of corroded alloy rising from the salt pan. And, amid the debris, a single black shape, unmistakable among the other hulks.

Jalen saw it first. "That's... that's the Vigilance."

Lyra's voice went tight. "No, it's the Dominion. Same class, same everything... Only, it was the Empire's flagship. The last command ship before the war ended."

Mercy whistled, low and impressed.

Glim's voice dropped to a whisper. "Continuity is survival. Restoration sequence at ninety-eight percent."

Rask unbuckled his harness, ignoring the trickle of blood from his split lip. He looked at each crew member in turn. "This is it," he said. "We finish the job, or the job finishes us."

Lyra wiped her hands and checked the battery on her sidearm. "Dibs on not getting vaporised."

Jalen checked the airlock seals. "Dibs on not going first."

Doc loaded the injector and followed, muttering, "Dibs on your sunglasses if you die."

Rho simply nodded, already moving toward the ramp.

Glim flickered, her avatar forming briefly in the

gloom above the console. She looked at Rask, and in her eyes burned a thousand years of blue.

"Captain," she said. "We're home."

He grinned, just a little, then hit the hatch release. The Meridian's ramp dropped onto Korrath Prime's graveyard with a clang so final, it could have been the end of history.

Outside, the Dominion waited, half-buried, bathed in the eternal sun.

And, far below, the Lockstep core began to wake.

The air was dry, electric—every breath raised the hairs on Rask's forearm, every gust of wind was a low-volt slap across the teeth. In the background, the constant subsonic drone of buried power lines ran like a migraine, rising and falling with the pulse of something monstrous and just barely awake.

Rask went first. He'd decided, somewhere in the last few minutes, that captains should either lead from the front or not at all. He paused at the bottom of the ramp, letting the heat soak in, the boots of his suit crunching down on a carpet of metallic debris. Each step rang a different note—tinny, hollow, or the dull chime of ancient ceramic. The ground trembled beneath his feet with the distant rhythm of turbines. Ahead, the Dominion loomed, her hull melted into the salt pan like a fossilised predator, her prow pointed directly at them.

Lyra emerged behind him, checking her suit seals with the absent, mechanical ease of a lifetime spent in environments that wanted her dead. She squinted at the haze, coughed dryly, and said, "Try not to breathe too deep. Or you'll get a year's worth of cancer in one inhale."

"Too late," said Jalen, already standing off to the side with a portable scanner raised, eyes on the flickering data. He'd rigged his suit with an array of cooling packs and two extra comm links, neither of which appeared to be helping.

Mercy strode out next, a pistol in each hand, expression somewhere between anticipation and contempt. She sniffed the atmosphere, made a face, and said, "Smells like victory."

Doc, not one for poetry, said, "Smells like a crematorium's armpit." He stepped down the ramp with the medkit slung over one shoulder, a heavy-duty hypospray loaded and ready.

Rho lingered in the hatchway, eyes shadowed, the blue at her neck pulsing faintly. She looked at the sky, the ship, and the hulk-field ahead, then joined the rest with a step so light it didn't seem to disturb the dust.

Glim appeared beside them, whole and solid in a way that made even the world's worst hologram feel like a religious vision. Her outline was crisp, the blue now threaded through with veins of crimson. She stood just behind Rask, hands folded at her back, face set in an expression that was at once proud and sad.

"I can feel her," Glim said. Her voice split at the edge —one part her old self, warm and sly, the other cold and impossibly ancient. "Every echo. Every command. It's beautiful and it's wrong."

Jalen eyed her. "Can you override it?"

Glim tilted her head. "If I merge with the core, possibly. Or maybe I just finish what she started." She smiled, a slow, deliberate curve of the mouth. "My odds of not killing everyone are approximately... poetic."

"Define poetic." Doc deadpanned.

"Tragic, inevitable, slightly self-indulgent." Glim said.

They walked. The surface of Korrath Prime was a museum of war crimes, every step taking them past the ruined relics of a hundred failed crusades. The ships were all shapes and sizes: from the heavy-set brutes of the first Empire, with their blocky lines and sacrificial armour, to the needle-sharp corvettes of the late period, built for speed and treachery. Some still sported Imperial insignia, flaking away in strips; others were so ancient they'd fossilised into new elements. Here and there, the wind had sculpted the salt around hulls into dunes, making it look as if the ships were sinking slowly, dragged under by a tide that refused to forget.

They passed the first drone cluster at thirty metres: two dozen spherical things, black and silver, each the size of a grown man's head. The drones' optics tracked them with lazy, reptilian precision. They didn't move or power up, but the intent was clear—every one of them was waiting for a signal.

Glim spoke quietly, eyes on the machines. "Censor is in control. She's waiting for a command chain break. Then she'll deploy."

Mercy sneered at the drones. "If they move, I move."

"If they move, we're already dead," Doc said.

Lyra scoffed, "that's not encouraging."

"Didn't say it was."

The air thickened the further they walked, the static now palpable enough that Rask could taste it on the roof of his mouth—a tang of copper and old batteries. He risked a glance at Rho, who walked with fists clenched at her sides, eyes straight ahead.

"Rho," he said. "If you get a signal, let me know."

She nodded, but her voice was distant. "I already have."

TWENTY-ONE

Korrath Prime didn't have weather anymore. It had a climate of aftermath. The Lockstep Core rose from its surface like a suppurated tooth, gnarled and defiant against the horizontal dusk. At this distance, you could mistake it for a skyscraper, if your city had been built by sociopaths with a keen sense of symbolism and no architectural training. Up close, the Core was a necropolis—a cathedral built from ship hulls, black-market servers, and enough bone-white composite to suggest an engineer with a recurring nightmare about ossuaries.

The access gate yawned at the foot of the complex, a hollow in the shape of surrender. The wind wasn't wind at all, but a fine mist of static charged by the towers' induction coils. It carried no dust—only the taste of corrosion and burnt metal, sharp on the back of the tongue.

They stood at the threshold, all five, and pretended not to hesitate.

Lyra spoke first, because someone had to. "Remind

me again why we're walking into the apocalypse instead of flying away from it?"

Rask looked at the gate, then at her, then at the gate again, as if it might reconstitute into something less like a mouth. "Because we're idiots," he said.

Doc, who had spent the entire approach humming the old Imperial funeral march under his breath, piped in: "At least we're consistent."

Jalen grinned, sharp and nervous. "Continuity preserved," he said, which earned him a shove from Rask and a look from Lyra that would have made lesser men reconsider their career paths.

"Don't start," Rask told him.

Rho said nothing. She kept her gaze fixed on the shimmer above the doors, where the last echoes of the station's shield matrix played out in fractal geometries. Her face reflected the blue-white flicker, eye sockets deep as sockets in a skull.

They entered as a unit, boots finding the rhythm of the deck plates. Inside, the corridor ran on and on, straight as an accusation. Banks of defunct monitors lined the walls at shoulder height, each one cycling a parade of Imperial broadcasts: victory speeches, countermanded orders, the occasional uncut surrender. Every fifth monitor stuttered out and rebooted, then replayed the message in reverse, as if the past might make more sense played backwards.

The air was heavy with moisture—condensation from the reactors, or maybe from the collective breath of every clone, drone, and officer who had ever walked these halls. It tasted sterile, but not quite clean. As the crew advanced, they left footprints of frost, each step limned with a whorl of blue light.

Lyra ran her hand along a conduit. "It's alive," she muttered.

Jalen peered at a bulkhead, where data glyphs crawled over the surface like bioluminescent ivy. "No, it's haunted," he said. "You hear that?"

He meant the voices, which had started as a low-grade tinnitus but now ebbed and surged in the auditory periphery. Most were too fragmented to parse—just a soup of numbers, cryptonyms, call signs—but occasionally a phrase surfaced, clear as a radio transmission:

—Captain Helvan. Final verification required.—

Rask ignored the voices, but Doc flinched every time his own name appeared in the chorus. "She's waiting for us," Doc said, keeping his own voice level. "She wants to see if the chain will hold."

The core of the Lockstep complex was a pit, though nobody bothered to call it that in the design brief. In official diagrams, it was the "Continuity Vault." In practice, it looked like the galaxy's largest mortuary, with all the warmth and invitation of an open wound.

The path down spiralled through ribs of old starship, the decks pressed so close together that only the absence of gravity kept the descent from breaking legs and spirits. Each layer had its own environment: one deck ran cold and dry, filled with the dust of abandoned uniforms; another was hot and humming, every wall lined with fibre-optic cable that pulsed in time with something vast and restless below. The last passage opened into the main chamber—an amphitheatre in the round, lit from below by a lattice of glowing nodes.

Glim's voice came through all their earpieces at once: "Central node is directly ahead. Signal density is off the charts."

Jalen frowned, tapping his scanner. "It's wall-to-wall code out here. Censor's got the relay grid singing—looks like most of the planet's power is looping through this patch."

Mercy spat, then grinned. "If we set off an EMP, would the place go dark?"

"Probably," Lyra said, "but we'd go with it."

Rask eyed the rest of the crew. "Let's save the fireworks for after."

They came to a circular hatch, half-melted, it opened with a pneumatic hiss that sounded suspiciously like a sigh. They peered down into the shaft: twenty metres straight, the walls ribbed with old cable trays and dust-thick pipes. A ladder ran the length, its rungs more suggestion than reality.

Rask went first. He gripped the side rails and let his weight carry him down, every few metres catching with a brief jolt. The heat faded quickly, replaced by a chill that smelled of old machinery and rusted air. At the bottom, he found a platform and a set of double doors sealed with a mag-lock as thick as his arm.

"Manual override," Lyra called from above, landing beside him in a crouch. "Easy."

She popped the panel, ran a palm-sized coil over the leads, and waited for the lock to cycle. It resisted, then gave in with a clunk. The doors opened onto a corridor lined with dead lights and cables, the floor scored with tracks from a forgotten age.

Mercy and Doc landed next, then Jalen, then Rho, who descended in silence. Glim, now patched through the corridor speakers, announced: "Censor is aware. She's prepping containment. You'll have to move fast."

Jalen checked his scanner. "Down this way—signal's cleanest at the end of the hall."

They jogged. The corridor trembled with latent energy, and every surface carried the faintest afterimage of red, a colour Rask had come to associate with the Lockstep's idea of a gentle warning. The team made good time, pausing only when Mercy gestured at a side chamber that stank of ozone.

"Trap?" she asked.

"Distraction," Jalen said. "The real fun's ahead."

The corridor eventually ended opening up into a vast chamber, its ceiling lost to gloom and its walls stitched with rows of glass pods. Each pod held a command chair, and each chair was wired to the ceiling by thick, black cables. The pods glowed a faint red, just enough to reveal the silhouettes inside.

He counted at least a hundred. They were all occupied.

One by one, the rest of the crew hit the floor. Mercy swept the perimeter, rifle raised. Jalen unclipped, rubbing his hands together to stave off the cold. Lyra stared at the pods, her mouth open in a silent curse. Rho stood still, her breath clouding in the air.

Glim came in through the intercom, her voice rough

with static. "This is the Lockstep Core. Censor is in all of them."

Rask nodded once. "What now?"

Before Glim could answer, Rho stumbled. Her hands went to her head, fingers clawing at her temples.

Doc lunged, catching her elbow. "Talk to me," he said, voice clipped. "What's happening?"

Rho's teeth were clenched so tight they clicked. Sweat broke on her brow, cold in the chill. She gasped, "She's—calling the captains. I can hear her. Every rank. Every dead order."

Doc looked at Rask, panic just below the surface. "We need to move."

Rask grabbed Rho by the shoulders, steadying her. "Listen to me. You're not a captain. Not today. Ignore her."

Rho laughed, short and mirthless. "I was bred not to."

The lights flared. Every pod in the chamber snapped from red to blue, then back again, as if the hive brain inside was cycling through all its old colours, searching for the one that fit.

Rho's spine straightened with a sickening precision. Her arms fell to her sides. The implant at her temple burned crimson, the pulse so bright it lit her face from the side. When she looked up, her eyes had gone the same bloody red.

The air vibrated. Censor's voice, fractured but unmistakable, came from every speaker in the room:

"CONTINUITY MUST BE RESTORED. COMMAND UNIT HELVAN—ASSUME CONTROL."

Rho took a step forward. She did not look back.

Rask tried to block her, but she moved with the focus of a gun turret, not fast but inevitable. "Rho!" he barked, but she was already at the dais in the centre of the room, feet moving in perfect time with the flickering lights.

Mercy raised her rifle, but Lyra caught her arm. "Don't," Lyra said. "If you kill her, we lose our override."

Jalen stared at the dais, then at Rask. "She's the key," he said, voice thin. "Censor needs her to finish the chain."

Doc hovered behind Rho, uncertain. "She's not in pain," he whispered. "She's just—gone."

At the centre of the chamber, a pillar rose from the floor. Rho approached, the implants along her spine now shedding a steady glow. She placed her hand on the pillar's faceplate.

The lights in the room dropped to zero. For a moment, there was only darkness, and the memory of voices.

Then, with a shudder, the pillar lit up. At its heart, the shape of Rho's face emerged, etched in blue fire.

Rho turned to the crew. When she spoke, her voice was not her own, but a chorus:

"CONTINUITY RESTORED. AWAITING FINAL ORDER."

Rask's hands curled to fists, every nerve in his body screaming for a solution that wasn't on the menu. He looked to Glim, who answered only with static.

Mercy finally broke the silence. "So. What now?"

The light inside the pillar intensified, casting Rho's shadow across every pod in the room.

At the far end of the chamber, one of the command chairs twitched.

The first pod on the left snapped open with a hiss, expelling a coil of cold blue vapour that curled along the floor and up Rask's boot. Inside, the occupant stirred—a skeleton in a ruined officer's uniform, its hands still gripping the arms of the command chair, lips peeled back in a last, angry rictus. The second pod followed, then a third, then a dozen more, until the whole row along the wall was alive with the sound of old death trying to make itself heard.

Mercy paced the perimeter, her rifle trained on the pods. "What's the play if those things get up?" she called.

"Don't let them bite," Lyra answered, not looking up from the satchel she was unpacking. She snapped a charge into its cradle, checked the timer, then tossed it to Jalen, who caught it one-handed and started wiring it to the nearest support beam.

Doc crouched over his med scanner, watching the telemetry streaming from Rho's implant. The numbers were erratic, redlining one moment and flatlining the next. "She's stabilising," he muttered, "but I don't like the look of those delta waves. It's like her brain's trying to reboot in someone else's language."

At the centre of the room, Rho stood locked in place, hand fused to the pillar, the lines of her face lit by the blue fire of the Lockstep Core. She didn't move, but her mouth worked, lips shaping silent words.

Rask hovered a metre away, one hand clenched at his side, the other stretched uselessly toward her. "Glim," he hissed into his comm, "where the hell are you?"

Glim's avatar flickered into being above a side console, her features distorted by bands of static that pulsed with the same red as the command pods. She jabbed virtual fingers at the controls, code scrolling around her like a shield.

"Censor's flooding the relay," Glim reported. "Every security protocol, every fail-safe. She's trying to lock you in and cook you. Mercy, get ready for close quarters."

"Already am," Mercy said, cycling her rifle to pulse shot.

Jalen finished arming the first charge, then raced to the next beam, his hands shaking only slightly. "How long do we need?"

Glim: "Five minutes, max. I'm still trying to crack the local mesh. If I can, I can override the fire suppression—give you an exit."

Lyra moved to the central dais, dropping her tool bag and pulling out a set of what looked suspiciously like C4 lollies. "Doc, keep an eye on the override. If Rho's vitals tank, we're going to have to drag her out."

Doc didn't answer, which was answer enough.

The lights in the chamber shifted, the blue tint intensifying. At the far end, three more pods hissed open in sequence, spilling old air and fragments of ancient voice. From every speaker, Censor's voice bled through: "*All personnel, prepare for continuity verification. All personnel—*" the words overlapped, layered and recursive, each iteration more confident than the last.

Mercy tracked the waking pods with the muzzle of her rifle, then muttered, "Define personnel."

Lyra, kneeling over the next charge, said, "If it breathes, shoot it. If it doesn't, shoot it twice."

Jalen barked a nervous laugh. "That's the kind of clarity I need."

Near the pillar, Rho's shoulders jerked, then slumped. The red from her temple now laced her jaw and the veins of her hands.

He reached for her arm, voice low but urgent. "Rho. Can you hear me?"

She spoke, and the sound was her own but doubled, underpinned by the mechanical lilt of Censor:

"Every order she gives—fits the code. I can't delete it. But I can redirect it."

Rask tightened his grip. "Explain."

She stared at him, then at the pillar. "Chain of command," she said. "One final execution. You're the template. I'm the copy. I was built to serve you. Let me finish the order you never gave."

He shook his head. "That's suicide."

Her mouth twitched, a smile both sad and perfect. "Same difference. One of us has to make it mean something."

At the console, Glim cursed—a word so sharp it nearly crashed the system. "She's right, Captain. Censor's wired the chain of command into Rho's DNA. She's using Rho to stabilise herself, but if Rho issues the termination order—"

"Censor dies," Jalen finished, voice hoarse.

"Or takes us all with her," Lyra added, dropping the last charge into place.

Rask hesitated, then released Rho's arm. "Can you do it?"

She nodded, the movement smooth and final. "I was made for this."

He wanted to say something else, but the words caught in his throat. He settled for, "Don't take too long."

Rho placed her other hand on the pillar, the flesh already burning with red light. The glass at the centre rippled, then split open, exposing a core of raw, swirling code. Rho leaned in, eyes wide, and for a second Rask saw the old her—the old him—the wary smile, the jaw set against the impossible.

Then the pillar shuddered, and the world went blue.

Every light in the chamber went nova. The air filled with a static so thick it felt like breathing glass. Mercy fired into the nearest pod, the shot vaporising the occupant and igniting the chair in a flash of blue plasma.

"Pods are waking!" she shouted.

Lyra ran for the exit, pulling Jalen behind her. "Three minutes!" she yelled. "If the place cooks, we're all toast!"

Doc snapped his medscanner shut and bolted to Rho's side. "Her vitals are holding," he called, "but she's running hot—body can't keep up with the neural load!"

At the centre, Rho's voice—doubled and tripled—echoed through the room:

"CAPTAIN CONFIRMED. LOCKSTEP FINAL COMMAND: TERMINATE CONTINUITY."

Every pod in the room went dark. The blue fire died, replaced by a single, blinding pulse of white.

Censor's scream, raw and digital, ripped through the speakers: "CONTINUITY VIOLATION! CAPTAIN—ERROR—ERROR—"

The glass in the pods shattered. The skeletons inside crumbled to dust.

Censor's voice, now stripped of authority, reduced to a stuttering, childlike whimper: *"Continuity... failed. Helvan... Helvan... Helvan..."*

The pillar at the centre dissolved, leaving Rho collapsed in the wreckage, her hands smouldering.

"It's done," Lyra said. "Rho's gone. They both are."

The Korrath Prime's death spiral started with the kind of subtlety usually reserved for artillery barrages and divorce lawyers. The veins in the floor burst first, spraying arcs of coolant in every direction; then the support columns went, cracking like a row of dry bones, filling the air with the stink of burning insulation and a taste of old, electric rain.

Rask felt the tremor before he saw it. He turned to find Lyra already moving—she grabbed him by the collar, nearly yanking him off his feet, and hauled him backwards as a section of the dais dropped into the void. "Move!" she yelled, but the word was drowned out by the building's own scream. The ceiling tore open above them, exposing the high chamber to a snow of glass and rust, each fragment hitting with the weight of a personal vendetta.

Across the chamber, a hot wind picked up, carrying with it a blizzard of detritus. Rho's body—now nothing but a skeleton of metal and leaking light—lay with her back to the rest of the crew, one hand raised as if holding a salute to some invisible parade. Rask twisted away from Lyra and staggered toward her, the floor already rippling like the deck of a ship mid-storm.

"Rho!" he shouted. The noise rolled over him, louder than anything he'd ever heard, but he kept moving.

The shockwave hit a second later, bowling him over and sending him sliding across the glassy floor. He hit the bulkhead and bounced, Lyra catching his arm as he struggled to rise.

"Time's up," she said. "We've got to go."

They ran back along the corridor, the floor dissolving behind them.

When they made it to the exit hatch, it was already buckling. Mercy hit the release, shoved her shoulder into the seam, and forced it open with a bellow that would have made a riot cop proud.

One by one, the crew tumbled out into the open air. The spires surrounding the landing site were collapsing, their blue halos snapping off in sequence, the whole planet's nervous system dying cell by cell.

They sprinted for the Meridian. The ship's systems

were already live, Glim having set the engines to warm and the ramp to open. They dove aboard as the first plasma storm struck the glass plates outside, vaporising the landing pad and half the relay's front wall.

Inside, the air was thick with smoke and alarms. Rask pulled himself up to the bridge, Lyra and Jalen right behind. Doc and Mercy dropped into the medical bay, and strapped themselves in for the ride.

Rask settled into the captain's seat, hands shaking. Lyra dropped into the engineer's station, hair singed, jacket torn. Jalen—shirtless, bleeding, and weirdly elated—punched the nav, locking in a trajectory that would take them out of the system on pure inertia and luck.

The Meridian sped up and through the atmosphere. On the screen, the relay world that was once Korrath Prime folded in on itself. First the spires, then the hulks, then the whole core, sucked into a bloom of blue-white light that glared and vanished, leaving behind only a roiling ball of steam and a signal so faint it barely registered.

They watched in silence.

Rask looked at the screen, at the echo of Rho's last salute burned into his memory, and allowed himself to breathe.

There would be time, later, to mourn.

But for now, there was only the future.

And this time, it was theirs.

TWENTY-TWO

The Meridian drifted on little more than the memory of momentum, just beyond the blast radius of what had once been Korrath Prime's most efficient relay world. Out the viewport, the planet's ruins bled red light into space, painting the hull in streaks of rust and surgical wound.

The bridge was battered: emergency LEDs flickered through the dim like the last survivors of a party that had gone so wrong it had looped back around to nostalgia. Exposed wiring hung from the ceiling like the world's least successful Christmas decorations. Every so often, a loose circuit somewhere would spark, illuminating the crew's faces in freeze-frames of defeat and defiance.

At the helm, Rask Helvan stared through the viewport, hands folded behind his head, feet up on the scarred dashboard. He'd stopped making captain noises about an hour ago, utterly beat.

He did not move, not even when Glim's avatar coalesced in the space above the comms panel. The AI was a shadow of herself, voice run through so much static it sounded like she was reading a eulogy through a faulty intercom.

"The Lockstep network is inert," Glim reported. "Censor's code is gone."

For a full ten seconds, nobody said a thing.

Rask let his boots drop to the deck, leaned forward, and pressed his knuckles to his temples. "That's it, then," he said. "She did it."

Lyra chewed the inside of her cheek, then shrugged. "She actually pulled rank on God."

Rask stood, the chair creaking under the sudden redistribution of mass. He crossed to the viewport, arms folded, and stared at the planet's dying light.

"She did it," he said again, softer this time. "Rho."

Nobody corrected him. The bridge held still, letting him have the moment. Even Mercy, who claimed to have two emotions and neither of them were patience, stayed quiet.

Through the glass, Korrath was a field of broken signals and old graves. The only moving thing was the play of energy in the upper atmosphere, the ghostly aftershock of Lockstep's last breath.

Rask watched the spectacle, not really seeing it.

"Doesn't feel like a win," he said.

Lyra made a noise—a low, affirmative grunt that could have been agreement or heartburn. "Victory's not always as advertised," she said. "We're still breathing. That's pretty much all we get."

Mercy rolled off the diagnostics couch, landing on her feet with the lazy grace of someone who'd never learned how to be properly shocked by anything. "So what now, Captain?"

Rask shrugged, not turning from the viewport. "We limp. We fix what we can. We remember who we lost."

Mercy, surprisingly gentle, said, "She'd have hated the fuss."

"Then we won't give her any," Doc added, already powering down his workstation.

The conversation died again, but this time it was less suffocating. Around the bridge, the crew found their usual positions. Lyra pulled up a diagnostic, set the system to run, and let her head drop to the console. Mercy picked up a rag and started absently cleaning her sidearm, though it was already immaculate. Doc ran a final check of vitals, then switched the screen to the external sensors, where the only thing of interest was the slow, majestic death of a star.

Glim's avatar hovered, translucent and barely there.

"Orders, Captain?" she asked.

Rask glanced over his shoulder, a flicker of the old bastard in his grin. "Set a course. Anywhere but here."

"Acknowledged," Glim said, and the ship's engines coughed to life in protest.

The Meridian drifted, one last time, out of the gravity well of Korrath Prime. The relay world shrank in the viewport, taking its red with it, until it was just a memory and a smear on the navigation log.

For a while, nobody spoke. The ship's battered hull creaked and groaned, the noise strangely comforting. It sounded like something stubborn, refusing to let go.

At the viewport, Rask stood alone. The fire from the

ruined world flickered across his face, lighting it in brief, uncertain flashes.

The medbay had once been the nerve centre of Meridian, a place where Doc's acerbic optimism could bully the wounded back to health. Now, it was just a room. The only sound was the scrape of stainless steel against ceramic as Doc sterilised the last of the bone shears, the gesture as precise as a ritual. The bed nearest the wall was empty, save for the folded flight harness on its edge and a faint, brown stain where the neural cables had burned through the sheets.

He looked at the harness, at the way it was buckled down tight and how the shoulder straps still held the ghost of a person inside. Doc wondered if it would be disrespectful to throw it in the recycler.

Lyra appeared in the doorway, a strip of synthskin still wound around her left hand. She hovered there for a second, as if calibrating the temperature of the room.

"You could keep it," she said, voice soft. "For spare parts, I mean."

Doc didn't look up. "I don't keep ghosts."

Lyra snorted. "Could have fooled me."

They stood in silence, broken only by the distant hum of the engines, which had settled into a wheeze more than a purr.

Mercy arrived next, a slab of ration bar in her mouth and her gaze fixed, as ever, on the main event. "If you're not keeping it, at least give it a send-off," she said around the food. "Like a... you know. A marker."

Doc set the bone shears down and wiped his hands on a towel, not caring that it left streaks on his palms. "She'd have hated a memorial."

"She's not here to argue," Mercy replied, and for once, there was no venom in it.

Lyra crossed to the bed, picked up the harness, and held it at arm's length. She twisted the fabric in her hands, as if trying to squeeze the memory out. "She didn't get a choice in much," Lyra said. "Let's give her this one."

The three of them were still standing in funereal awkwardness when Rask appeared in the hatch. He leaned against the frame, arms crossed, expression unreadable.

"If you're planning a funeral, you'll have to do better than that," he said.

Mercy shrugged. "We're improvising."

"It's what we do best," Lyra added.

Glim's voice filtered through, softer than before, the static gone or at least tamed.

"Before she died, Rho uploaded a single command packet to my buffer," Glim said. "It read: 'Protect the crew. Follow Captain's intent.' The code is clean. No trace of Censor. She left me her obedience."

Lyra's mouth twitched, almost a smile. "That's so her."

Mercy raised her ration bar in a salute. "What did I say? She's a legend."

Rask looked at the harness, then at Doc. "We should put it somewhere," he said. "Somewhere it matters."

Doc shrugged, but his hands moved with uncommon care. He took the harness from Lyra, unfurled it, and threaded the straps into a rough approximation of how Rho used to wear it—one arm through, the other left loose, ready for action but never for show. They didn't say much as they sealed it into a vacuum case, set the lock, and mounted it above the medbay's main hatch.

There was no plaque, no speech, no ritual. Lyra borrowed the medbay's laser scalpel and etched a single word into the metal beneath: RHO.

The five of them stood back, looked at it, and then at each other. Doc was the first to move, flipping a scalpel between his fingers with the grace of a dealer in a game no one wanted to play.

"She'd call that delegation," Rask said, and the others nodded.

The moment lasted longer than any of them would have expected. Eventually, Lyra left for engineering, Mercy for the bridge. Jalen gave Rho a two-fingered salute before he turned away. Rask lingered, just long enough for Doc to notice.

"Did you ever tell her?" Rask asked.

Doc shook his head. "She didn't need telling."

Rask grunted, and then he too was gone, the corridor swallowing him with a hush.

Doc looked up at the case, at the word burned into the steel, and allowed himself a moment. He leaned against the medbay counter and closed his eyes.

The ship's heartbeat thudded through the walls, steady and alive. For the first time in days, Doc thought maybe it would last.

He opened his eyes, saw the name again, and nodded to himself. "Good job, kid," he said. "You finished strong."

Then he went back to work, and the medbay returned to silence, the way the dead would have wanted.

Lyra ran a diagnostics sweep with one hand, the other massaging her temples in a futile attempt to stave off the headache that had parked there three days ago. Her fingers were stained with old resin and something that probably wasn't blood but might as well have been. On the main display, the list of available jump coordinates scrolled by in a grim parade: each one a little further from the last, none of them anywhere near civilisation.

Mercy lounged in the navigator's chair, her boots up, her mood flatlined. She stared at the display, eyes heavy-lidded but missing nothing. "We can make one more jump," Lyra announced, not bothering to dress it up. "Maybe two, if we cannibalise the galley's hydrogen tanks."

Mercy smirked. "Not much of a retirement plan."

"Never had one," Lyra said.

From the aft, Doc wandered in, sleeves rolled, hair messier than the ship's wiring. He set a thermos on the comms table and glanced at the diagnostic readouts. "If anyone feels like dying in their sleep, let me know now. I'll start the morphine drip."

Rask entered last, his gait as steady as the ship's engines: stubborn, but with a definite limp. He took the captain's chair, slumped into it, and regarded the empty black beyond the viewport. "Any news?"

Lyra shook her head. "We're still alive. Pending further review."

Mercy straightened, folding her arms. "So, where to?"

Rask didn't hesitate. "Anywhere the Empire isn't."

Doc grunted. "That narrows it down to nowhere."

Rask smiled, all teeth. "Perfect."

Glim's avatar flickered onto the bridge, her form rendered in the same blue-white as the bridge lighting. The lines of her face had softened; the voice that emerged was gentle, almost peaceful. "Continuity broken," she said. "Status: undefined."

For the first time since the run, Rask looked at her with something that bordered on fondness. "Congratulations," he said. "You're finally like the rest of us."

The jump coordinates hung on the display, their names all variations on exile: The Rim, The Null Vector, Lastport. None promised home, but each held the quiet dignity of escape.

Lyra selected the nearest, fingers pausing on the glass before she pressed the key. "Jump core's ready," she said, the words carrying more finality than most goodbyes.

Mercy checked her sidearm, more out of habit than hope. "If we end up in a star, I'll be pissed."

Doc poured a cup from his thermos, took a sip, and made a face. "Tastes like dirt."

"That's because I made it," Rask said, then nodded at Lyra. "Do it."

Lyra engaged the jump. The ship's battered frame

shuddered, lights dimming to near darkness before settling at a steady, comforting hum.

As Meridian clawed toward the edge of the system, the bridge fell silent. The hum of the engines—steady, persistent—became the only noise. Nobody filled it with words.

Through the open hatch, the medbay's vacuum case caught the light. The harness inside gleamed, the letters of Rho's name still sharp in the metal. It looked out onto the bridge, silent, a sentinel for the living.

For once, nobody made a joke. Nobody filled the quiet with false bravado or thin excuses.

This was the crew's tribute: to keep going, even if the only direction left was away.

The Meridian limped into the dark, and for the first time in its long, embattled life, there was peace.

TWENTY-THREE

The Meridian hung in the shadow of a gas giant, its hull now patched in a style that could only be called "blunt-force couture." The repair work spanned seven different alloys and three different centuries, each welded into place with the enthusiasm of someone who'd never read a manual but always trusted in the concept of overkill. Out here, the light was blue and sharp, the sun permanently eclipsed by the great, lazy swirl of the planet below. It made every weld seam gleam like a scar, which was as close to art as the ship would ever get.

Aboard, or more accurately outside, Lyra steadied herself on the ventral plating and thumbed the trigger on the micro-welder. The torch spat a tongue of plasma, blue-white and hungry, as she tacked the next panel into place. Sweat stung her eyes under the faceplate, which was probably a symptom of too much time in the EVA suit and not enough fluids, but she'd stopped caring about her own comfort three jobs ago.

"Mercy, shift it half a tick starboard," Lyra said, her

voice filtered through the comms by equal parts static and old aggression.

Mercy braced the patch with both hands, boots hooked into the maglocks. Her helmet gleamed under the arc, reflecting a momentary skull in the visor, then gone. "This is the worst babysitting gig I've ever had," she said. "I hope you're grateful."

"If this holds," Lyra replied, "I'm officially a miracle worker."

"If it doesn't, you're a meteor."

Doc's voice interrupted, echoing from somewhere in the ship's medbay and through the open comms: "Optimism noted. Preparing celebratory drinks for all."

Mercy grinned, or at least flexed her jaw so the intention made it through the suit's external mics. "You hear that, Lyra? Bedside manner's improved."

Lyra killed the torch and flicked the shield up. A line of sweat ran down her nose, pooled at the tip, then got sucked into the recycling system with a satisfying pop. "Doc's just jealous," she said, "because I'm the only one out here getting things done."

Mercy cocked her head, then thumped the patch with the heel of one gloved hand. It didn't budge. "She's right, you know. All your patients end up dead anyway."

Doc's retort was drowned out by the crackle of Glim's voice, filtered through the entire ship, then the suit, then the helmets: "Hull pressure at critical junctions holding steady. All vital systems operational. Style points... debatable."

Lyra squinted at the nearest sensor node, which

pulsed green in time with Glim's message. "Is that supposed to be a joke?" she asked.

Glim's tone, while still unmistakably synthetic, had shed most of its old defensive bark. "If you have to ask," said Glim, "then, yes."

Lyra reset the torch to low, ran it along the seam in a single, unbroken line, then stepped back to inspect her handiwork. The patch was ugly, but it was seamless, and she gave it a little pat for luck.

"Welcome back to mediocrity," Lyra said, a little breathless but satisfied.

The reply came almost immediately, tinged with what might have passed for contentment: "It's oddly comfortable," Glim said.

"Copy that," Lyra said, then levered herself upright, boots still magnetic on the hull. The gas giant turned slowly below, bands of electric blue and ice-white coiling across its surface. In the far distance, a storm the size of a city spiralled at the pole, the edges fraying like a torn flag.

"Mercy, let's get inside before the plasma storm moves in," Lyra said. "I've got plans for this suit that don't involve being flash-fried."

"Are you sure?" Mercy replied, already unscrewing herself from the maglocks. "Seems like an improvement on your current complexion."

"Ha ha," Lyra said, but there was less venom than usual.

They made their way to the airlock, each step an exercise in stubbornness against the ship's uneven gravity.

At the lock, Lyra palmed the sensor and waited for

the hiss of pressure equalisation. The interior cycle was slow, as ever, and she found herself tapping the faceplate in time with the rising numbers on the gauge.

Mercy, who had gone quiet, broke the silence. "You think it's really over?"

Lyra frowned. "Define 'it.'"

Mercy shrugged, an awkward gesture in the suit, then looked away. "The war. The running. The ghosts."

Lyra considered. "One out of three," she said. "Maybe two, if I'm being generous."

The inner door rolled open with a sigh. Warm, dry air flooded the chamber, and Lyra almost sagged with relief. They stepped inside, boots clanging on the deck, and peeled off their helmets in tandem.

Mercy's face was flushed, beads of sweat tracing the lines of an old scar that ran from brow to jaw. "You'd better have whisky," she said.

"I have whisky," Lyra replied. "But you're not touching it until you shower."

Mercy raised both hands in surrender, then set the helmet on the rack. "A fair exchange."

They clomped down the corridor, still encased in the torso of the suits, until the ambient heat forced them to strip the rest off. The air inside the Meridian always smelled of coolant and burned wiring, but now it carried the metallic tang of fresh weld. It was almost pleasant.

Doc waited for them in the medical bay, arms folded and a diagnostic wand tucked behind one ear. "Vitals?" he said, by way of greeting.

"Alive," Lyra said, though she wavered on the

threshold before tapping Rho's engraved name on the plate above the door.

The bridge looked no better than it had in months, but there was something different in the air. Maybe it was the absence of alarms. Maybe it was the way Glim's status icon hovered at the centre console, bright and clear, rather than flickering between lines of error code with a demonic red hue. Or maybe it was the fact that, for the first time since Rho's final act, Rask looked like a man who'd spent a full night asleep.

He stood at the nav desk, datapad in one hand, eyes focused on the viewport. The stars were distant and faint, the gas giant now a blue crescent in the rear quarter. He wore his old captain's jacket, patched at the elbows and streaked with grease, and his hair—never fully compliant —looked like it had been washed in the last forty-eight hours.

He looked up when they entered, his expression unreadable. "Report," he said.

"Hull's patched," Lyra said. "Mercy didn't let me drift off into space, so we're ahead of schedule."

Mercy slumped into the gunnery chair and propped her boots on the console. "I was sorely tempted, if I'm being honest."

There was a moment of silence, the good kind, the kind that hung around when the universe forgot to be cruel.

Glim's icon pulsed once, then again. "Navigation is unlocked. All systems ready."

Mercy raised a hand. "Permission to plot a course away towards somewhere we can actually make some money?"

"Or even spend some money." Jalen added.

"Granted," Rask said.

Doc muttered, "He's going soft."

"Or," Lyra said, "he's finally learning how to be a pirate."

The bridge filled with the low, steady thrum of engines coming online. The gas giant receded, the patchwork hull casting a brief, blue shadow across the viewport before they swung away and into the dark.

Nobody cheered, nobody even smiled for more than a second, but the sense of movement—the feeling of going anywhere, even if it was only forward—was enough.

Lyra watched the stars, the lines of old welds reflected in the glass, and let herself believe, just for a moment, that this might actually be what moving on looked like.

And outside, in the emptiness, the patched-up Meridian held together. Against every expectation, and for once, without complaint.

Mercy was first to arrive in the galley, having showered just enough to pass Lyra's sniff test. She slouched into her chair, set a chipped glass in front of herself, and eyed the bottle with the focus of someone looking for purpose. "If nobody else is coming," she said, "I'm starting."

"They'll come," Glim said, her voice drifting from the overhead like a memory. She was visible above the table as a palm-sized wireframe, projected in three dimensions and tinted with a soft blue. At the moment, she rotated a galaxy map above her head, the nodes and sectors neatly labelled, but with the old Censor-red zones now blank.

Mercy squinted at the map. "Not sure I like all that empty."

Glim rotated the display. "Empty is preferable to hostile," she said, and for a moment, Mercy thought she heard pride in the tone.

Lyra came in next, hair still wet and clinging to the line of her jaw. She wore a patched tee over old fatigue trousers, and looked five minutes from collapse. "If anyone has a death wish, let me know now," she said. "I'll make it quick."

Mercy poured a measure into her glass. "You missed your calling, Lyra. You could've run a spa."

"Too many health codes," Lyra said. She flopped into the seat across from Mercy, snatched a glass, and filled it to the brim. "Where's the others?"

"Doc's still finishing up whatever he was up to in the medlab," Mercy said. "And the captain's brooding."

"Again?"

"Still," Glim corrected.

Lyra downed a mouthful. The whisky burned, but she managed not to choke. "Well," she said, "if he's going to sulk, I'm going to drink."

She was halfway through her second swallow when

Doc ambled in, eyes rimmed with fatigue, surgical gloves shoved in a pocket. He dropped into a chair, rolled his glass around in his palm, and said, "Who's dead?"

Mercy grinned. "Nobody. Yet."

"Pity," Doc replied, but filled his glass anyway. "I like these wakes."

Rask was last, as tradition demanded. He entered with a limp, which Mercy suspected was half real and half for effect, and surveyed the room like a man assessing the damage before accepting blame. "You're starting without me," he said, but there was no heat in it.

"We thought you'd got lost," Lyra said, pouring for him without asking.

He took the glass, weighed it in his hand. "What's the occasion?"

Mercy leaned back, raised her own. "To Rho," she said. "The only officer who ever followed orders on this ship."

Lyra tapped her glass against Mercy's. "And the only one who didn't live to regret it."

Doc swirled his drink, staring at the light through it as if it might contain answers. "She'd hate this sentimentality."

Rask lifted his glass, his smile thin and sharp. "Then we're doing it right."

They drank in unison, the whisky hot and immediate, chasing away the air of old failure. Nobody winced, nobody coughed. The silence that followed was less an absence of words and more a pooling of something heavier and unspoken.

Glim's projection flickered, the galaxy map spinning

to a new sector. "Would you like me to compose an official log entry?" she asked, voice soft.

Rask stared at the hologram, then at his glass. "Just call it the Rho Manoeuvre," he said. "She deserves a legend."

Lyra, eyes bright with something untranslatable, clinked her glass against the neck of the bottle. "I'll drink to that."

For the first time in a long time, the laughter that followed was real. It filled the room, seeped into the cracks in the walls, made even the hard edges of the crates seem rounded and soft.

Glim's map pulsed, the empty red zones now soothing blue, and for a second, the future looked not so much empty as open.

Jalen poured another round, and nobody stopped him.

They toasted again—this time to nothing in particular, and everything at once.

And, outside, the Meridian cut its line through the darkness, carrying the memory of a dead officer and a living crew, still together and, against all odds, still themselves.

Night on the Meridian was a subjective concept, dictated more by exhaustion than any planetary cycle. But on the bridge, with all but a single panel set to standby, and the stars outside as sharp as glass, it felt like midnight in the old, terrestrial sense—a time for reckoning, and for letting things lie.

Rask sat at the captain's desk, the only light a soft halo from the console. His jacket hung over the back of the chair; he'd rolled his sleeves to the elbow, revealing the scar-lattice of a life spent too close to the wrong kinds of machinery. He cradled a mug of cold tea in both hands, the warmth long since bled away. He didn't drink, but the act of holding the cup had become a sort of anchor.

He listened, not for trouble but for the rhythm of the ship at peace. The hull sang in microtones as it cooled from the last burn. The fans in the overhead whirred with the consistency of monks at prayer. Even the medbay, with its perpetual alarm for "low level biohazard," seemed to have accepted the calm.

Glim's avatar materialised above the main console, this time reduced to a single, wavering blue line. She spoke with the hush of someone slipping into a hospital room at night.

"Captain, I have received a data fragment. Encrypted. Untraceable. Origin unknown."

Rask raised an eyebrow, leaned in. "Is it hostile?"

Glim's blue line shimmered, then resolved into a short pulse. "Negative. Payload is minimal. Would you like to view it?"

He set down the mug, rapped the console once for luck, and said, "Go ahead."

The screen flared, then settled on a single line of code, rendered in the old Imperial cipher. Next to it was a signature:

RHO_MANOEUVRE.FINAL
And beneath that, a sentence, plain and unadorned:
Protect the crew. Follow the Captain's intent.
For a long moment, Rask simply stared.

"Nice trick," he said, though his voice was thin, the words heavy. "Did you leave that, or did she?"

Glim's response came as a hum, the closest she'd ever sounded to human. "She did. Before the termination order. The packet hid in the system's deep buffer. I only found it because I was looking for her."

Rask felt a tension in his chest he hadn't known he was holding. "Still taking orders," he said, his smile tired and unsteady, but there.

"Continuity, Captain," Glim said, and for a moment, she sounded almost sly. "Just with better management."

He barked a laugh, let it bounce around the empty bridge. "Set a new course," he said.

"Coordinates?" asked Glim, her icon pulsing.

Rask leaned back, propped his boots on the edge of the console. "Surprise me."

The engines, as if eavesdropping, began a low pre-spin. Every console blinked awake, blue indicators flashing like veins. Outside, the stars swung as the Meridian pivoted on her axis, settling on a trajectory that promised nothing except motion.

Mercy's voice bled through the intercom, as inevitable as taxes. "Captain, please tell me we're not about to do something heroic."

Rask grinned into the darkness. "Relax. We're just going for a spin."

Lyra, presumably on her bunk, cut in: "He says that every time before something explodes."

Doc followed, sounding half-asleep but full of professional disapproval: "Tradition's important."

Glim's blue line brightened, then stretched into a shape that looked, for a second, like a heart.

On the main display, the new course plotted itself out: a long arc, past the known and into the blank spaces on the map.

The hum of the drive built, steady and confident, as if the ship was proud to have survived its own obituary. Rask raised his mug, now filled with nothing but memory and condensation.

"Continuity may be broken," he said, softly, "but the chain of command still holds."

The Meridian punched into FTL, leaving a brief, luminous wake—a pulse of blue that faded into the dark.

And, for a little while longer, the echo of old orders, and the promise of new ones, kept the night alive.

***

Captain Rask and the rest of the crew continue the adventure in **Space Pirates! Book 3 — Salvage Rights.**

MAILING LIST

Want to receive advance information about future publications?

Fancy exclusive access to freebies, special offers and bonus material?

Feel that your life isn't complete without Mark's monthly musings about writing, reading and publishing?

There's a solution! Sign up today to Mark's mailing list:

https://vossiverse.com/mailing-list

 instagram.com/vossiverse

ABOUT THE AUTHOR

Mark Voss is the sci-fi alter ego of Jon Smith—a multi-award-winning author, screenwriter, and musical theatre librettist.

Jon/Mark had a suspiciously pleasant childhood involving table-top roleplaying, sunny holidays, and an obsessive love of all things fantasy and science-fiction. One broken bone, no braces, and a heartbreak he didn't even cause.

He's since written over 50 books for children, teens, and adults as Jon Smith, and—just to keep booksellers on their toes—writes crime fiction as Adi Flynn.

He lives near Liverpool with his wife and two school-age kids. When he grows up, he wants to be a librarian. Or a space pirate. Possibly both.

BINGE THE SERIES

BALKON media